THE
DREAM
KEEPERS

MARTY PRIEST

DEDICATION

To Justin Alt and all children who believe.

CONTENTS

Acknowledgments   i

Chapter 1--- Everything Happens In A Hollow Tree   Pg. 1

Chapter 2 --- A Slip Of The Tongue   Pg. 7

Chapter 3 --- He Has Mental Powers   Pg. 11

Chapter 4 -- The Ancient One Appears   Pg. 17

Chapter 5 --- The Land With Two Suns   Pg. 27

Chapter 6 --- A Fantastic Journey In Oberron   Pg. 39

Chapter 7 --- Fishing In The Dark All Night   Pg. 57

Chapter 8 --- Mother's Painful Memories   Pg. 69

Chapter 9 --- The Spirit In The Pantry   Pg. 73

Chapter 10 -- His Name Is Abraxas   Pg. 77

Chapter 11 -- Saving The Poor Fish   Pg. 85

Chapter 12 -- An Indian Head Penny   Pg. 93

Chapter 13 -- The Secret Room   Pg. 99

Chapter 14 -- The Book Of O   Pg. 105

Chapter 15 -- Ice Cream With A Wild Girl   Pg. 111

Chapter 16 – Tangled Thoughts   Pg. 125

Chapter 17 -- He Becomes A Character In The Book   Pg. 131

Chapter 18 -- The Blue Stone   Pg. 145

ACKNOWLEDGEMENTS

A heartfelt thanks goes to Dr. Galen Boehme for editing without hesitation or judgment, Lorilee Maxwell who read my story as I wrote it and smiled, Russel Woodworth whose computer savvy saved me, Mary Scott for supporting always, Carrie Tice, a bright spark of inspiration and Rene Alt that saw the big picture.

CHAPTER ONE

Twigs snapped beneath his feet and the wind tore at his clothes as Nicholas ran down the steep hill. He stopped abruptly at the bottom, gasping dumbfounded. A gnarled and broken old tree grew where never before by the creek! How could it be? This was his favorite spot. He'd never seen this tree before, though he'd been there just a couple of days ago. It had suddenly appeared out of nowhere. Never in all his twelve years had such a thing happened. The tree looked like it had been there forever.

He walked toward the tree slowly, the moment magnified by disbelief. Something strange had happened here. A presence surrounding the tree drew him toward it and gave him chills up the back of his neck, though the warm spring sun shone brilliantly overhead. A sacred power, far beyond his own, overwhelmed him and brought him to his knees on the grass. God, the tree was beautiful! Though the tree looked dead, he admired its twisted and splendid bulk that looked as if it had been struck by lightning. Blackened edges near the jagged top made him think it had been on fire. He tried to memorize every detail in case the tree decided to disappear.

Bursting with curiosity, he got up and walked over it. The rough bark felt very real to his palm as he placed his hand upon the trunk and walked slowly around the tree, his hand trailing behind him. Up above, the cracked and splintered trunk pointed to the electric blue sky. Sitting calmly on the only branch, a large brown owl inspected him with a pair of unblinking yellow eyes. The owl surprised Nicholas and stopped him dead. He felt that he intruded upon the owl's privacy. The owl swiveled his head from side to side in a broad sweep of the countryside to survey the land.

Nicholas felt privileged, knowing full well that owls didn't often show themselves to people in the middle of the day. The big bird adjusted its wings as it shifted its weight from one foot to the other, settling down in a low squat. It looked straight at Nicholas. He thought it asked one silent question. "Why are you here, young one?"

Nicholas answered the owl silently in turn, "Because I love this place."

The tree and the bird were one, their patterns of browns and grays matching perfectly in a grand camouflage that had almost made him dizzy. When he looked down, a lump of astonishment swelled in his throat at the sight of a large black hole in the tree trunk.

He leaned into the hole and looked down as far as he could. It just got deeper and darker. His hand broke loose from the rotten wood and he lost his balance, and then caught himself. A cloud of golden dust shimmered in the sunlight. Goosebumps popped out all over his skin. Something funny was going on. This just didn't happen every day. He'd never felt quite this way before. He felt nauseous, tired and bewildered. How could the tree be there? He sat down with his back against the trunk and wiped his thick blonde hair from his sweating forehead.

Blackbirds cackled nearby. On the other side of the creek, a chubby brown squirrel leaped between two locust trees. Beyond the woods, a thick field of wheat like an ocean of green waved in the wind. Though he noticed all these things it was almost as if he wasn't there, like none of it was happening. Maybe he'd better lie down. His body fit snug inside the nest of gnarled tree roots. Yes, perhaps he could accept the appearance of the tree. What did it matter? What did he know? Weird things always seemed to happen to him. Within moments he fell fast asleep.

Nicholas dreamed that he traveled deep underground, boring like a mole through thick soil where worms wiggled and beetles burrowed. Somehow he descended through thick layers of limestone that glowed with a warm light growing brighter as he sank deeper and deeper into the Earth's crust. He knew something good was about to happen. He could always feel that sensation. Finally, he popped through the rock into a huge crystalline cavern. Hundreds of dagger-sharp stalactites hung from the ceiling and contorted stalagmites like misshapen creatures grew up from the floor. It was like being at the center of the Earth. He was completely protected. No one could bother him or even find him. No one could...

The scraping sound of rock upon rock startled him. It came from his left where a crack in the wall had appeared. The rocks parted further and slid open wide like a door, the heavy grating sound echoing about. His heart jumped when he saw standing in the opening a tiny old dwarf.

The dwarf smiled knowingly at him as if he had expected Nicholas. The dwarf's dark eyes blazed with fire as he sang a bold melodic song.

We have returned here at this hour
To kindle the flame of nature's power;
That strength that grows each passing day
Will crack the stone and awake the clay

The inspiring tune lifted Nicholas so that he felt a tingling on his bare arm. A small green plant sprouted from his skin! In fact as he concentrated on it with his mind, the plant quickly grew into several full-fledged flowers that blossomed orange, green and blue. How amazing. He could grow plants with his mind!

The sound of tinkling bells and soft chanting voices drifted toward them. He expected the dwarf to say something, but the curious fellow just smiled even wider, then spun about in place and jumped into the air with a click of his hob-nailed boots. This amused Nicholas greatly, so much so that he fell on the cavern floor laughing. The earth felt moist with kindness. He rolled ecstatically from side to side and back again, the motion erasing all of his cares. He giggled and bubbled with joy, gaggling like a goose with surprise.

When Nicholas looked up, a group of colorful dwarves stood in a circle around him. They began to sing and play a beautiful song upon tiny instruments. One bright faced child in crimson shirt and knickers held a drum between his knobby little knees. He beat it precisely, leading the rhythm of the symphony. A young lady in crystalline dress of white gossamer played upon her twelve stringed harp with the grace of one blessed from birth.

An old geezer dressed in rags wheezed upon a silver flute, his nimble fingers dancing delightfully upon it. The look of warmth on his face, on all their faces touched Nicholas. These dwarves were his family. The children laughed, or did they sing? He couldn't quite tell. Their faces beamed and their eyes held such happiness. Never had he seen such a crowd. One man lay on his back with his feet dancing in the air and his hands clapping at all the right moments. The words of their song brought tears to Nicholas' eyes.

> Take a look inside your mind
> And you might find a friend of mine,
> That friend is you that friend is me
> Together in this mystery.

He felt relieved and grateful to be in the presence of such splendor and charm. A new sensation welled up in him though, a disquieting sadness emanating from somewhere down the tunnel. He got up from the cavern floor and walked down the tunnel deeper into the Earth. The music had stopped. Everyone looked sober as they walked beside him in silence, the clippity-clap of their tiny footsteps echoing off the rock walls. The tunnel became wider and higher as they went, until finally it opened up and they entered another huge cavern. In the center of the dimly lit place, he saw a large shimmering pool. Suddenly he knew he was dreaming even as he stood transfixed before the still water. Three words came to mind, "The Meeting Place."

A vision stirred, and then took shape on the surface of the pool. Tall buildings, skyscrapers in a huge city covered with a dingy blanket of smog blotted out the sun. People below on the windswept sidewalks and asphalt streets hurried helter-skelter, their pensive faces drawn with displeasure and animosity. The sight struck him as odd, then gripped his guts and threatened to awake him from the peculiar dream. Nothing could be worse, people without a true purpose, people insulated, not by thick rock walls of a beautiful cavern, but by the glass and iron structures they had created without thought of their effect upon the land.

He had to do something about it. That was why he had the vision. No one could tell him what to do or show him the way through. Only he could find a way. These simple folk, these small but grand dwarves around him all understood why he needed this vision. They were a part of him, a part of the spirit of understanding that he longed for. He looked up at their concerned faces. They felt as he did about the Earth. Something needed to be done.

A small boy, so much shorter than the rest, gazed into the pool, his clear green eyes intent upon it, his body as still as the water. His golden curls about his glowing face lit up by the vision gave him a holiness that awed Nicholas. Nicholas had to see more, though he didn't want to look.

The images in the pool shifted and he felt an awful fear. Countryside appeared, but not one like his healthy homeland above. No beautiful trees or sparkling river graced this land, just the barren wire-fenced enclosure of a desolate dark skinned people. Hundreds of men, women, and children sat or lay listlessly about on the hard dusty ground. Most of them wore the shabby western clothing of hand-me-downs and cast-offs, while others wore very little. Their swollen bellies and gaunt features screamed starvation. Troublesome flies buzzed about and crawled all over their exposed limbs and faces. Dark-glazed eyes looked hopelessly to no one.

Those weary looks of displeasure ate at Nicholas' conscience, burrowing in like a wounded animal seeking a place to hide. This starvation had to stop. He didn't want to look. Why was this happening? He had so much to eat that it befuddled his senses to see them in such a sorry state.

No one in the crowd around him at the pool said a word. He knew they all watched. He had to do something. He had to help.

One woman in the vision held her crying child so close to her sunken breast with arms so thin and frail that he though her arms would snap. How could their poverty and suffering go on? He had so much in his life. They had so little.

Nicholas awoke from the dream even hotter than when he had fallen asleep. The sun now shown with a vengeance upon the little spot beneath the tree that was once shaded. His face felt tight and burned as he yawned and raised himself up on his elbows. Man! That was some dream. His life had a way of turning strange just when he thought he had it figured out. Nothing like this had happened to him before though, not quite. This was different.

He felt groggy, as he stood up, the dream still fresh in his memory. So much of the dream was good, so inspiring and surprising. And yet the visions in the pool disturbed him deeply. He couldn't decide which the stronger emotions were, but he had to tell someone. They had to know. The world was in trouble and something had to be done. He could do something he knew. He could feel it in his heart. He walked at first, and then ran, jumping over logs and darting through the tall weeds and up the hill.

CHAPTER TWO

The sun hung low in the sky by the time Nicholas reached his house. The long walk to town had tired him, but his mind churned with ideas and questions. He jumped up the front step, opened the screen door and slinked through in one fluid motion. Quietly, he stepped from the hallway to the living room, his sneakers soundless on the hardwood floor. He couldn't wait to tell his mom about his adventure.

She sat on the far end of the sofa in the living room and didn't look up when he entered. A magazine laid spread out on her lap. One hand held her head in her favorite thinking pose, the one that always amused him, her thumb beneath her chin, her two longest fingers pointing precisely at her jaw and cheek bone and the back of another finger just brushing her lips. As he sat down beside her, a slight crease at the corner of her eye became a crow's foot that signaled she acknowledged his presence.

"Mom," he said softly.

She let out a long sigh. "Hold on," she said without looking up. "I want to finish this article on dreams." She held the corner of one page gingerly between two fingers as if it contained something very important.

"Mom, you wouldn't believe what just happened," he blurted out.

She gave him a pained look as one strand of her brown hair dropped comically to her furrowed brow, then returned to the magazine. "Just let me finish this," she said with finality. He squirmed about and nervously stuck one hand down the crack between the soft cushions. She could be so difficult sometimes, like trying to talk to a statue.

He slid down off the couch to the floor on his knees and watched her. Her steel gray eyes were so intent upon her reading that he couldn't help being drawn into her thinking. Sensing her thoughts seemed so natural now that he had let go of his expectations. He studied the lines on her face. She certainly looked old. She had told him that she didn't ever remember her dreams. So why did she have this sudden interest? The more he waited, the more he realized the importance of the article to her. He could feel her need to get something from it.

"What does it say?" he asked quietly.

She began to read like one enchanted. "Down the tunnel, down the long tunnel they walked, their eyes darting from side to side in the darkness, looking for the way."

Wow! That sounded like his dream. This was really strange. She continued on. "Dreams are like memories. Their symbolic meaning comes to us when least expected to show us something or help us to release tension and anxiety."

The room spun about him for a few seconds. The picture of the hound dogs sitting at a card table playing poker that hung over the fireplace, the kitchen doorway, even the blue carpet beneath him all seemed to turn like a merry-go-round, then stop. The floor lamp cast a yellow light over his mother who went in and out of focus. He couldn't keep his mind from merging with hers. Her thoughts somehow became his.

She read more. "Our unconscious minds know exactly what we need to see, hear and feel..."

He finished the sentence. "... in order to make whole those fragments that haunt us or reflect upon our daily affairs." His mother looked shocked. She grabbed his arm and squeezed it with a roughness that startled him. "How did you know what I was going to say?"

He was beside himself, truly. This was so strange. It had just happened, like in a dream. He hadn't meant for it to be this way. Her question made him uneasy. She looked demanding as if he'd done something wrong.

"I don't know," he stammered. It just happened. I must have read that magazine in school." He could tell that she didn't quite know if she believed him. She even looked a little angry. "We had a lecture in school about dreams," he said. "I must have heard it then."

She slapped the magazine closed and rolled it up into a tight cylinder. He had to get out of there. There was no way he could tell her about his dream, not now, not like this. Her agitation made him think that she wouldn't believe him. The sight of his muddy sneakers gave him a plan. "Oh dang, I better get out of these wet shoes." He hopped up from the floor and headed for the stairs. As he shot up the steps, three at a time, he felt her eyes boring holes in his back, but she didn't say a word.

In his room, he felt dejected. His blue and white striped sailor shirt itched all up and down his back with prickly little seeds, so he pulled it off over his head and tossed it into the corner. The tired old box springs squeaked in agony as he flung himself on his back onto the bed. He raised himself up to his elbows and looked around. Everything felt flat and lifeless. His erector set display of buildings on the desk held no interest. His big poster of a magnificent buffalo standing alone on the open prairie gave him no comfort. The nightstand next to his bed held his collection of unusual rocks that offered no help. The alarm clock said six o'clock straight up.

His newfound ability to read his mother's thoughts had backfired. Her reaction frightened him. He didn't understand.

9

Something inside of him was changing and though a part of him felt excited about the prospect that quickly sank beneath the heaviest of thoughts. He was an alien. No one could help him either. He was just too weird. Nicholas clutched the covers and stared up at the swirls of the plaster ceiling. Outside his window, a tree branch scratched against the pane.

Funny how he knew his mother wouldn't understand. Dreams scared her. Though she read about them, she couldn't do what he could. She didn't see things as he did. His new power told him that it was so, just as it had told him how to finish her sentence. This new ability was a curse. It helped him to know things, but the more he knew the harder life became. The burden weighed upon him like a huge weight on his chest. Tomorrow, he'd go back to the hollow tree. Maybe he would find some answers.

CHAPTER THREE

School dragged slowly by for Nicholas the next day. The warm spring air made him drowsy as he sat at his desk by the open window, thinking about the old dwarf.

Occasionally he'd look up at his teacher Mrs. Morrison who stood in front of the blackboard before the class. Once in a while, she'd give him a dirty look, because she knew that he wasn't paying attention. He did notice that much. It took all his will power to keep from jumping out the window and running as fast as he could to the creek. Playing at the creek always made him feel good. In nature he could relax where nobody would bother him.

Some of the other children didn't look so interested in the lesson either. School could be boring, especially today when he wanted to be elsewhere. He could feel the teacher thinking about asking him a question as she wrote on the blackboard in a smooth cursive hand. She always did that when she sensed he wasn't listening. He had no idea what she wrote, but he found himself compelled to watch. She was all right. He had no real problem with her. He just didn't feel like paying attention to the lesson.

Her bushy silver hair looked dry and seemed to float on her head as if filled with static electricity. The jiggle and sway of her sagging arms fascinated him as she wrote. How could she stay so serious for so long? She wore an antique flower printed gray cotton dress that barely contained her rather large body. As she stepped from side to side, her weight shifted from hip to hip with an awkward bounce. He giggled to himself. Sometimes she looked so silly. He liked her though. She could be a lot of fun at times.

The old dwarf popped into his thoughts again. Nicholas wasn't so sure about his new mental power, but he still wanted to explore the workings of his mind. Perhaps if he thought hard enough, he could make something happen. It was worth a try. He chose a spot on the back of Mrs. Morison's head and concentrated upon it with all his might. It seemed like a useless exercise, but you never knew. Thinking about only one thing for a long time could be quite difficult. The more he stared at her head though, the more he kept thinking of the ancient dwarf. He couldn't help it. Thinking about the dwarf made him happy. He decided to stare at Mrs. Morison's head, but think only of the ancient one. This was not only fun, but he also began to feel energized and giddy. Before long, he felt that the back of her head occupied the very center of the whole room.

Then his focus shifted. To his surprise, he noticed that she had taken the chalk from her right hand and now she wrote with her left, something she had never done before. At first he thought it peculiar, but not nearly so much as the squiggly letters that she began to make. She spelled out loud as she wrote, "Capital T, y, c, o." After the last letter, she made a dramatic circular sweep of her arm and underlined the strange word twice.

Nicholas' concentration broke completely when she turned around toward the class, horrified. He felt a twinge of guilt. Obviously she didn't like what she wrote. Had he made her write the word? She looked right at him then, right through him actually, as if she knew he had. Just as she opened her mouth to speak, the recess bell clanged and the children jumped up out of their seats. He felt glued to his chair as they all stampeded for the door. His best friend Freddy was the last to leave. He tossed Nicholas a fearful look over his shoulder. Then he too was gone.

Mrs. Morrison looked embarrassed. Of all things, she didn't like being embarrassed. He was in deep trouble; at least he thought he was. She walked over to her chair, sat down in it and clasped her hands together on top the desk. That singular pose usually made her look so regal, but not today. He could tell she was disturbed even though she looked impassive. One of her cheek muscles twitched several times. He had never seen it do that before.

He felt sorry for her. How could he have done such a thing? As weird as it seemed, he knew that he had made her act so strangely. There was no other explanation. He had to make it up to her if he could. She looked sad as she sat there staring at nothing, so he got up from his seat and walked toward her. He could see a tear in her eye now. Perhaps he could help, but to do so meant explaining his experiment on the back of her head to her. He wasn't so convinced that he should do that.

She looked at him then, the role of teacher coming upon her. "What's wrong Nicholas?" she asked. "I've never seen you quite so…"

Flustered, he shrugged his shoulders and picked up a pencil from her desk. He tapped out a rhythm with the eraser head, hoping against all odds that he could leave and have everything be all right. That was unlikely. This was one of those moments he dreaded with adults. They held all the power, or so it seemed.

"Now I know your father's hard on you sometimes," she said, "but that's not what's wrong, is it?"

A pain stabbed at his chest at the mention of his father. Nicholas always tried to forget him since he couldn't understand his father's meanness. The pain faded though as he looked into her soft gray eyes. He shook his head no and pursed his lips. This explanation for his being distracted was no simple matter. Where should he begin? He rubbed the pencil shaft hard with his thumb and stuck his other hand into the pocket of his blue jeans. God, life was hard! He had to split. She wouldn't understand. She was friendly and everything, but her mood could always shift, especially if she learned about what he had just done. Maybe it was all just nonsense. She was in control. He was confused.

The word "Tyco" popped into his head. It sounded so familiar. Then he knew. Tyco was the name of the dwarf, the ancient one. The insight gave him hope. "I think I know what Tyco means," he said without looking up.

"What on Earth is that?" she asked incredulously.

Their eyes met and Nicholas knew he could trust her. She didn't have any anger or judgment against him. All he could see was compassion welling up like the tears he saw ready to fall if he didn't explain. She had more than a teacher's concern. She had the real experience of his condition. That much he now knew.

"It's the name of a dwarf that I dreamed about," he said relieved. She smiled and got up from her chair. As she walked around the desk and sat on the front of it next to him, he was glad that she was his teacher. Perhaps they could even be friends. She wiped her eyes with the back of one hand and placed the other on his shoulder. His face felt warm and flushed. When she withdrew her hand, he cleared his throat and spoke. "I never knew it till now," he began, "but when I think about something real hard it can affect things, like the way you wrote his name on the blackboard." He looked at her with some small sense of authority. Perhaps he had what she needed. The thought encouraged him.

"You mean you think you had something to do with making me write Tyco on the blackboard?" she asked. "Do you think Tyco is the name of your dwarf friend?"

He smiled. Now he knew for sure that it would be okay to tell her everything. His story spilled out in a stream of enthusiasm that surprised even him. The tale all came back to life as he told her what happened at the creek and what he learned about the mysteries deep beneath the Earth.

Mrs. Morrison took everything in without blinking an eye. At the end, she looked pleased. She walked over to the blackboard and traced the chalk lines under the word Tyco with her index finger. "So Tyco is your dream pal," she said touching her hand thoughtfully to her cheek. When she removed it, a thick line of white chalk trailed across her deeply tanned skin looking like Indian war paint. Nicholas burst out laughing. She could be so endearing.

Her eyes sparkled as she wiped at the chalk and smeared it even more, and then sat back down on the edge of her desk. She crossed her arms over her bosom and gave him a challenging look of amusement. "Have I got a story for you," she said as she smoothed her long dress down over her knees.

He sat down in one of the small desks in the front row, his elbows on the wooden top and his hands curled over it to the cool metal front. Her story ought to be good. She had that look that made students want to listen, like the fate of the whole world depended on her words. "When I was quite a bit younger than you, I had a friend like yours. I called her Summer. She wasn't a dwarf or anything, but she had a way of showing up at the funniest times. I still remember clearly how elegant she was. Her blonde hair fell about her shoulders in long tresses and her face always seemed to light up when she spoke."

Mrs. Morrison looked doubtful then, like she too was afraid to confide in someone. Her dilemma moved him. "Do you still see her?" he asked.

She leaned forward to inspect her ankle and fingered a tear in her hosiery. "Oh my gosh," she exclaimed. "I have another run." She pulled away the thick fabric with a sigh, and then let it snap back into place.

There was more here than she wanted to tell. Nicholas could see that much. A misty look came over her, and then she grimaced and shook her head no. "I guess I'll never see my friend Summer again." She stared out the windows, somewhere far away. "You see that was the whole problem in a nut shell. No one believed that Summer was real. I was the only one that could see her. My father made me think that I was bad. He said I shouldn't lie like that and pretend there were invisible people around me. But that was a long time ago."

Mrs. Morrison looked at him so intensely, that he felt a sudden flash of heat at his vulnerable position. "You have a chance, Nicholas. You could make a difference. Don't ever think that your dreams aren't real or what you believe in isn't important. Our dreams and beliefs are all we really have."

Her words echoed about in his mind. For the first time in his life he knew that he couldn't let anyone stop him from living his dream. People didn't always understand what you did, but if you let their opinions and judgments hold you back, you were doomed. He had to be careful, but he had to be true. Nothing else mattered to him. That was the only way he would ever uncover the mysteries of the Earth.

CHAPTER FOUR

he lost souls of the Earth need you. Alarmed at the strange words in his mind, Nicholas awakened totally from a half-sleep. That was the best time for messages to come to him. Often, he heard similar messages, each one just as striking and concise.

He rolled over and pulled the tangled sheet, damp with perspiration, away from his body. In his dreams the night before, powerful earthquakes had shaken the Earth to its core. Mountaintops exploded everywhere, flinging boulders through the air, but he had sidestepped each and every one of them unscathed. The map of the United States had a bite the size of several large states chewed out of the West, the whole area sinking like the Atlantis of old beneath the pounding tidal waves. Millions of people had drowned.

The morning sunlight streamed in the window and reflected off the metal buildings of his erector set on the desk. The Earth had to purify itself. People had abused and mistreated her for far too long. Upheaval could be the way, unless they listened more to God and each other and changed their ways. The words in the "Earth Song" came back to him. "The power that grows each passing day will crack the stone and awake the clay." The song must be a warning of sorts, but when might it all come to pass?

Maybe he worried too much. His concern lived somewhere deep inside him, a distant but constant companion. Occasionally it would surface and shout out to be heard, like this morning. Then he'd have to listen.

Some people were lost, their souls wandering, the blind leading the blind. You could see it in their eyes, though they appeared to have everything under control. They could pretend that they weren't in pain and it didn't matter that they abused and polluted the Earth, then forget that they pretended, convincing themselves that their lives were better than they were, but he could not. He couldn't help feeling responsible for the Earth.

The toothpaste tasted like wet clay as he brushed his teeth before the bathroom sink down the hall, something he didn't usually do first in the morning. He needed to cleanse himself though. In the mirror, his likeness looked grotesque. His oily hair had poofed way out on one side and laid squashed flat on the other, while his brushing made his cheek bulge. His reddened eyes showed a lack of sleep, but their blue centers held a firm resolve that struck him. Something had to be done, but what? Even Mrs. Morrison couldn't tell him that. She only knew what he had told her. He must be crazy for thinking he could do anything that would really matter. What could one twelve-year-old boy do anyway?

He went back to his room and sat on the bed. Today was Saturday at last. Going out to the creek would cheer him up. As he put on his clothes, he wondered what he would find at the creek. First, he brought out a clean t-shirt from his dresser drawer, then his faded blue jeans which were so worn and familiar. When he pulled them on he felt ready for anything. He appraised the holes in the heels of his socks. His mother often pleaded with him to let her darn them. That wouldn't do. It took all the magic out. She just didn't understand. He brought out his black and white sneakers from beneath the bed and slipped them on. The long frayed laces held true as he pulled them tight. Yes, this day held promise.

Sucking in an enormous breath, he stood on his tiptoes before the dresser mirror and flexed every muscle he could find in a contorted grimace that made him laugh. Nothing about him looked that tough now. He wasn't exactly the Hercules type, just a thin wiry creature, and one that could think quickly on his feet. He liked being himself. Even though life could be hard, he never lost his sense of humor. He bugged out his eyes, scrunched up his nose and snarled, then laughed again. God, he was silly. He knew that he could be deadly serious too, but his playfulness would never die.

Outside, a fresh breeze blew across a cloudless sky. Spring looked inviting with its fine layer of dew sparkling on the grass in the yard and the hedge all around it.

It took less time than before, to travel from the edge of town to the crest of the hill overlooking the river. He left his bike at the top and looked down at his domain. His favorite place looked pretty much as it always did, except for the hollow tree standing solid below. The steep slope flew by as he ran at top speed down the hill. At the bottom, he slowed and meandered over to the creek. Several sparrows chirped noisily in a willow thicket beside him. From a dead tree across the creek, a red headed woodpecker fired off a volley of rat-a-tat-tats that gave him a pleasant surprise. Nicholas searched among a large pile of creek rocks, head bent downward, absorbing every bit of the surrounding landscape through his pores. This place was special.

By the time he reached the old hollow tree, he felt tired. The trip from town always did that to him. Funny how he'd never noticed the tree before the other day. It appeared to be such a part of the land, as if it had always been there. Eventually he'd get used to it, like everything else. He picked up a long stick and twirled it like a baton. He belonged here. Nothing could stop that feeling. It was his secret. It wasn't just the creek by itself that attracted him or the trees or the birds for that matter. There was something else here, a hidden force moving in everything that he wanted to know. To know that force must be the main reasons that he was alive, though for what other purpose, he couldn't be sure. If only he could share these feelings with others.

He took off his daypack and lowered it to the ground, where he sat cross-legged at the base of the tree. As he unzipped the top of his pack and pulled out his recorder, he thought about his younger brother Ethan. Suddenly, his heart pounded and raced. It had been a long time since he had played the instrument, not since the day his brother Ethan had died. The recorder had lain untouched on Nicholas' dresser ever since. Ethan had given him the recorder as a birthday present just a few days before he drowned in the Mississippi River way up north several years before. His little brother hadn't even known how to swim. How he missed Ethan so.

The smooth mahogany instrument felt good in his hands as he leaned back against the tree and gingerly placed his fingers upon the air holes. The first few notes came out stifled and disjointed, but after a few moments, he began to play one of his favorite songs. The delightful melody and his memory of the words gave him a sense of relief that he always loved.

Waters ripple and flow
Flowing swiftly to the sea
Bring my freedom to me
Set my spirit free
River Hura flowing
Flowing swiftly to the sea
Bring my freedom to me
Set my spirit free

He played the song over and over for quite a while, swaying with the rhythm and the feel of it. After a long while, he quit playing and continued to hum. His throat vibrated with the rich soothing sounds rising from within. He closed his eyes, hypnotized. His head felt lighter and a floating sensation came over him as the vibration traveled downward into his chest, making each of his long slow breaths a gift to his body. The chant grew with strength of its own accord. His breathing slowed even more, becoming a circle so smooth that he couldn't tell if he inhaled or exhaled. Never in his life had he had quite such a sensation.

When he stopped humming, the trickle and hiccup of the creek felt comforting. The warm sun thawed his insides completely. He placed his palms on the ground. The fingertips of his left hand pulsed slightly as they sucked nourishment from the Earth. The essence of the land flowed into him, coursing through his veins and pumping through his heart, filling him with a vibrant charge. His awareness expanded even as a part of him dived inward deeper and deeper into the waters of his own being that he found so seductive and sweet. His head lolled back then and his mind soared.

Up out of his body, he rose. It felt peculiar and a bit awkward to be separated from his body sitting below him on the ground. Somehow, he'd managed to escape. His heart leaped when he looked to his left and saw Tyco sitting precariously on the branch of the hollow tree, his wrinkled old face radiating an enchanting wisdom. He stood up and balanced himself on one leg like a stork wobbling about, then with all the agility of a fairy leaped into the air and whooshed past Nicholas.

The sheer force of Tyco's flight spun Nicholas about. At first Nicholas couldn't control himself, but when he focused his mind on a spot just between his eyes, he found that he could slow himself down, and then stop altogether. In fact, he could even fly through the air now. The more he concentrated, the faster he flew. It wasn't long before he caught up with Tyco who had already flown far down the winding creek that looked like a tiny silver snake glittering in the sunlight below them. He could fly. He could actually fly!

Nicholas was contented to go where Tyco bade him, but when the ancient one put his hand on Nicholas' shoulder and they suddenly appeared before the hollowed out tree, Nicholas was shocked. Tyco knew a thing or two. He was magic!

Tyco continued to surprise. He grabbed Nicholas by the hand and jerked him along behind him, down into the hole of the tree. Nicholas wanted to scream with joy, but he didn't even have the chance to think. The tree roots formed stair steps leading ever downward far into the Earth. Tyco's crescent moon belt buckle gave off an eerie glow that lit up the tunnel as they passed layer after layer of crystalline white quartz and amethyst so purple.

The tunnel seemed to go on for miles, though time itself might have been suspended. The journey gave Nicholas great satisfaction, while the beauty of the place transfixed him as they passed through larger and larger caverns. In one of them, a circle of stalagmites grew up from the cavern floor, created by the purest of white mineral deposits dripping down upon them. The tiny frozen figures could have been a bunch of pixies or elves facing their leader, a larger mineral deposit whose widespread arms gestured welcome and greeting. The leader of the mineral group had what looked like a wide brimmed hat tilted at a friendly angle to one side and a long pointed nose that dripped a milky colored liquid to the cave floor, forming the cutest little shoes with up-turned toes. Nicholas only had a moment to see the stone figures as Tyco and he passed by, though he wanted to linger. Nicholas wasn't sure whether the figures were alive or not. The little leader almost seemed to be when his green eyes sparkled and looked right at Nicholas.

Tyco walked on ahead through the cavern. Nicholas didn't want to be left behind, though he felt that he would have liked to see more of the amazing rock figures.

Each cavern that they passed through was more beautiful than the last. He couldn't help but feel that some incredible designer had constructed the caverns with careful attention. He wanted to sing with happiness, but out of respect for Tyco's somber presence, he kept silent.

Something about the trip through the caverns felt different from his dream journey. The suspension of time, above all else, tipped him off. On his last trip, they had traveled down similar corridors of stone, but he had the distinct impression of time passing. He felt disoriented. Were they going back into the past or forward into the future? His disorientation grew, but Tyco remained unchanged, his eyes straightforward, glazed with intention.

The tunnel twisted and turned. Nicholas felt energized. Somewhere down this corridor he would find something that would take him back to the past, a far distant past that he would gladly remember. A softening in Tyco's eyes indicated that something good was about to happen. From out of thin air, their destination came to his mind in three simple words; The Meeting Place. They were going to the Meeting Place.

Finally they entered a cavern so huge that Nicholas couldn't see the rock walls or a ceiling, just darkness all around. Tyco's belt buckle light had gone out. Fear rose in him for a moment, and then passed. No, it would be too easy to give into it. He had to be brave or the whole trip would be pointless.

A pinprick of light showed up then, somewhere far in front of them. As they got closer it grew and his excitement mounted. Something was about to happen, something of great importance. That single thought drew him forward beside Tyco. How could anything bad ever happen with the Ancient One around?

The pinprick of light became much larger, now a flattened oval shape that glowed bright with promise. Tyco and he both walked faster, Nicholas skin prickling with anticipation.

Dark shapes appeared in front of the light; the silhouettes of what might be people, moving about with a purpose he couldn't make out. The light had grown much larger. Nicholas could now see that it was actually a huge lake shimmering from within. The endless lake filled the cavern floor and disappeared somewhere far off in the distant blackness.

Nicholas ran toward the dark shapes that he now knew were people. They all raised their arms high in unison, their palms facing him in a grand salute. These weren't just people! They were the little ones, Tyco's friendly troupe of dwarves from Nicholas' dream!

The crowd bunched up close together, thirty or forty of them, waiting for him. He ran at top speed, feeling mischievous, certain that the group welcomed his arrival. Just before he reached the crowd, he took a mighty leap up as high as he could and landed smack dab in the middle of the little people. They fell like dominoes, first one then another, until every one of the dwarves lay sprawled about, limbs tangled together, laughing and screeching with delight.

Nicholas raised himself up on his elbows and tried to get comfortable on the hard cavern floor. The dwarves lay about in a tangle as if they did it all the time. Between the bent elbow of an old man and the raised knee of a younger one, Nicholas recognized a face, the young blonde-haired boy from his dream. The boy had stood beside Nicholas then, gazing into the pool of terrible visions. The boy's face looked cheery, a bright and shiny smile playing lightly upon it.

"Hello, Nicholas," the boy chirped. "We've been waiting for you. What took you so long?"

The boy's question made Nicholas laugh. The troupe of dwarves laughed with him, a rich and vibrant sound that echoed about the cavern. By the time Nicholas had stopped laughing, the dwarves had all disengaged themselves from each other. They squatted on their haunches, hugging their knees with their arms, watching him, an attentive group that looked like rockets ready for the launch.

The little boy squatted with the rest, his tiny chin resting on his arms, his eyes aglow with curiosity.

"How did you know my name?" Nicholas asked.

The boy licked his lips all around in a circular motion as if the movement helped him to think. "Oh, we've known for a long time," he said. "We have a funny way of knowing who's who." The boy looked about at the others in the group, then back at Nicholas.

"What's your name?" Nicholas asked.

The boy squeezed his nostrils shut with two fingers in what looked like an attempt to dam his thoughts up inside his head and then darted his eyes from side to side as if looking for the answer. "David," he finally replied, "but my friends call me Bill. With a smile, he added, "you can call me Willing."

Nicholas didn't know if Willing kidded him or not, but he certainly liked the name. Willing suited the character of the boy. Nicholas found the unabashed openness of the rest of the dwarves just as charming. They were hard to understand completely, but he knew them to be genuine. The mysterious dwarves tickled him endlessly, but made him think as well. They didn't spell everything out for him. He wanted to talk with the dwarves, but he didn't know where to begin. Their presence overwhelmed him so, though he felt quite welcome.

"Can you imagine what it would be like if you couldn't talk?" Tyco asked, inching forward in a duck walk so he could see Nicholas better.

Nicholas thought about the question for a few seconds as he got up on his haunches and squatted like the others in the group. "I guess so. Sometimes I think it would be better that way."

The little boy stood up and stretched with his arms up high over his head, then walked slowly over to the sandy lakeshore and looked down into the water. The silvery light from the lake lit up his innocent face. Suddenly, the light turned blue, a strong but gentle and mesmerizing color.

Nicholas got up and walked over beside the boy. Looking down in the lake gave him a surprise. His reflection, if his it truly was, looked much older by at least ten years. It couldn't be himself! When he moved, his reflection moved too. His reflection had much longer and darker hair and a mature face with a pronounced jaw. The person reflected in the water also wore the same faded Levi's and white t-shirt he had put on that very morning. It was him! He had become a grown-up!

Nicholas stumbled forward with a splash into the water that rippled outward. Suddenly, he knew he was dreaming. Once again he had awakened within his dream without returning to his body. The realization only made everything around him all the more real. Something or someone approached from far off in the water, their presence growing as the waters lapped gently upon the shore and the group of dwarves crowded in around him and the boy.

A string of clear thoughts touched upon Nicholas' mind. "Hear these words, my peaceful brother." The silent message flowed from his mind and into his heart, demanding his attention. Then he saw the maker of the message and his mind swam in its beauty. At the bottom of the lake, a silken amber creature lay curled on its side like a newborn. It had a large oblong shaped head with two big brown eyes and a long slender body with small graceful arms and webbed fingers. Nicholas shuddered with recognition. He knew this creature. As strange as it seemed, he knew that at one time, in some ancient place, he had looked just like it. The creature probed into the recesses of his most private thoughts and gave him a vision.

Two great suns, one fiery red and the other bright yellow, blazed down upon an aqua colored planet. Majestic mountains jutted up through layers of blue and green clouds. Beneath the mountains, at the bottom of a turquoise ocean, a dome-shaped temple made of silver and gold radiated the whitest of lights from the center of an amazing underwater city. This was his home, a place so wonderful and familiar that he cried at the sight of it.

CHAPTER FIVE

Though Nicholas loved the episodes with Tyco, his elation could only last so long. The other kids at school and especially his best friend Freddy hardly talked to him anymore. He often found his experience with people in what they called "The Real World" disappointing. Most people feared anything beyond their five senses. He was, it appeared, developing a sixth sense; one that took him places in his mind where others didn't want to follow. His parents thought his musings silly. Every time he mentioned a dream or a vision, they changed the subject or told him he was too analytical and scoffed at him with a disdain he found disheartening.

After reading a book called "The People Down Under" from the city library, he grew even more restless. The Australian aborigines held such a high regard for their dream selves and dream lives that they couldn't comprehend why the white people thought dreams unimportant. In Dream Time, many things could happen. One could experience what the Aborigines called The Real World. Even many Native Americans went on a vision quest, a sacred ritual designed to bring the adolescent seeker special knowledge of their life's purpose. That sounded so great to Nicholas. He felt left out; although he knew many children or young adults had the same problem. Heck, even the parents seemed lost in their lives.

Sometimes his mom seemed to care about how he saw things. She made him think that she was interested in his deeper thoughts, but she just humored him so she could get him to do something for her. He usually didn't realize it until later though, after he had already been sucked in by her promise of understanding.

Nicholas didn't know whom to talk to. None of the other children his age seemed very interested in his otherworldliness. If they had really known him, they wouldn't fear him so much. They'd join him in the simplest things, like laughing at jokes, biking around town, and going fishing or just hanging out and doing nothing in particular. He hadn't really wished for the unusual dreams, at least he didn't think so, but now he had to understand them.

Lying on his stomach, on the floor of his upstairs bedroom, he drew a colored pencil map of Europe and thought about Lucy, the girl from across the street. She had shown a peculiar interest in him lately. He had known her for years, but for some reason now, whenever he turned around she would be watching. The other day, when he had passed by her house, she stood on the other side of the fence and stared at him. That gave him the chills. For some reason, he thought she expected him to do something, but for the life of him he couldn't figure out what. Her unusual beauty made it harder to concentrate. Her thick long black hair and alluring black eyes, even the smoothness of her skin, all made his attraction for her unbearable.

He didn't know a lot about girls one way or another. Other than school, his experience was limited mostly to playing an occasional game of neighborhood dodge ball or a dirt clod fight in which someone almost always wound up getting hurt.

Girls could be so troublesome too. The older he got, the more he found that to be the case. Sometimes they would tussle in fun during recess or after school, just a way to explore each other. That could be fun. But one girl had attacked him outright in the school hallway. It had happened only a week ago, late after school, when no one else was around. He remembered coming out of the sixth grade classroom minding his own business, when Terri Kesstler showed up.

Terri carried her books close to her chest in front of her as she approached. Her thick long straight blonde hair, combed perfectly in place, framed her pretty face. When she spotted Nicholas, she gave him a witchy smile like she wanted to eat him. Terri's aggressive tendencies knew no boundaries. It wouldn't be wise to let down his guard with her.

"What are you wearing to the dance?" she asked, walking along beside him down the hall.

Nicholas cringed and shrugged off the question. He didn't know how to answer. Her questions always made him want to run, though they had had a few fun times together with Terri's brother Craig who had been the same age as his brother Ethan. Being alone with Terri was a lot more dangerous. She always tried to corner him into something he didn't want to do. Lately he had to avoid her as much as possible. It seemed she followed or found him every chance she got. He knew that because he did feel her pain and was somewhat attracted to her. She would cling to him and torment him with her strange tomboy ways.

"My mom said she wanted to take our pictures when you come pick me up," Terri said giving him her full attention. He looked straight down the hall that all of a sudden seemed really long and dark. He had never told her he would go to the dance with her. In the sixth grade, bizarre things happened to you. A girl like Terri could make up a fantasy all in her head that had nothing to do, well, very little to do with reality, and then try to trap you with it. Some of the other boys had nicknamed Terri, Spider Girl. That name seemed to fit.

His only crime in the past with Terri had been to be nice to her, something that could get him in trouble quicker than almost anything. Oh sure, he had talked to her about the dance, since she had quizzed him forever about the dang thing. He didn't even want to go to the dance. Why did sixth graders even have dances anyway? If it hadn't been for their music teacher, Mrs.

Cane, they wouldn't have them at all. She thought them so important because music made you cultured.

The thought of going to the dance with Terri bothered him. Some small part of him thought it might be fun to get close to her. Her physical charms were somewhat appealing at times. He pursed his cheeks until they squeezed his tongue. She wouldn't like it if he said no to her. That would be the worst thing one could do to someone like Terri Kesstler. He jammed his hands in his pockets and tried to be invisible, though the click-click of her patented leather heels on the floor tiles distracted him. His whole body began to ache, anticipating trouble. Terri Kesstler had been known to be a little crazy.

"Would you like to carry my books?" Terri asked, offering them to him. Nicholas took them automatically, knowing only afterward that had been the wrong thing to do. Terri bristled with pride. She held her head high and flared her nostrils, which accented her large but well-formed nose, then stuck out her chest, making her small protruding boobs strain tight against her blouse. Her reactions surprised and flustered Nicholas. Terri could be attractive to be sure.

"I bought a new pink dress especially for the dance," Terri said heatedly."

Now Nicholas knew more than ever that he was in trouble. He had to stop it all before the situation got even more ridiculous. "I'm not going to the dance with you," he said somewhat softly.

Terri grabbed his shoulder and pulled him to a stop. "What did you say?" she asked in disbelief. Her face had suddenly turned red and she looked livid with rage, her eyes wide with panic.

Nicholas knew she would erupt at any moment. His problem just couldn't be helped. He had gone this far and now he had to finish it. "I said I'm not going to the dance," he blurted forcefully.

Terri looked so outraged that Nicholas pulled away from her grip and began to walk ahead of her. It didn't take long for her to catch up though. He could hear her approaching at a run behind him. Just as he stopped and turned, he saw Terri rearing back with one leg, preparing to kick him with all her might. His instinct took over then. He dropped her books and took one long step backward just as she kicked out at him. He grabbed her foot and raised it high until she fell backwards and landed on her butt.

Her skirt had flown upward, exposing her bare legs and a pair of blue cotton panties that she quickly covered, though she looked shocked, her face now bloodless and white. Nicholas watched her scramble to her feet feeling pleased that he had been able to protect himself. She probably had no idea that he could undo her so easily. His satisfaction was short lived though. Terri came at him like a cat and scratched him viciously across the back of his hand. She then scooped up her two thick books and tore off down the hallway, leaving him amazed at her wildness, holding his painful bleeding hand up for a look. She had scratched him good, a long straight gash that oozed bright red.

Nicholas lay on his bedroom floor and thought back on the incident. His hand had almost healed completely already. With a green colored pencil, he traced the long thin scab where Terri had scratched him. Oh, well, it had only hurt for a little while. Funny how some girls acted. He looked from the encyclopedia he laid out on the floor in front of him, and then at his map drawing for geography class. It had started to look pretty good. Eastern Europe had turned out better than he had expected, the squiggly borders matching the picture in the encyclopedia where he had traced them well. Now all he had to do was fill in the colors of the countries.

As he filled in the borders of Hungary with a solid red, his mind drifted back to Lucy, the fourteen-year-old neighbor girl from across the street. Now there was a girl, quite different from Terri Kesstler. But would Lucy be as much trouble as Terri?

He wondered at the sound of footsteps coming up the stairs. When the door opened and Lucy entered the room, he panicked.

"Thanks, Mrs. O'Malley," Lucy said with her hand on the doorknob, looking back at his mother who was already descending the stairs. Nicholas never had a girl in his room

31

before. He continued his work as if she weren't there, though she sat down beside him on the floor. That made concentration impossible.

"What are you doing?" she asked lightly, propped up on one arm, her hair hanging dangerously close to his face.

"Just drawing this map for geography class," he fired back without looking up. The silence that followed didn't seem to faze Lucy. She acted as if they had been best friends forever and she visited all the time. Her sweet-smelling perfume clouded his mind, making him draw like a drunk. His brown pencil shading of Yugoslavia had spilled across the border into a green Hungary. If Lucy noticed the mistake, he couldn't tell, but he had to fix it. It wasn't like him to lose control so easily.

He chanced a glance at Lucy and wished that he hadn't. Tears streamed down her face. He picked up a pink eraser and tried to fix his mistake on the paper. What could be wrong with her? What was he supposed to do? The brown overlapped shading smeared under his eraser and looked a terrible mess. Two hours of work wasted because of Lucy and now he had his hands full with her. He put down the pencil and leaned back against his bed.

Lucy sniveled, the tears continuing without any end in sight. He got up and walked to the bathroom down the hall. A tissue might help. He didn't know what else to do and was halfway down the hall before he realized he had left her alone in his room without an explanation. No one ever cried openly at his house.

After he returned and handed her the Kleenex, he sat down on the floor again, feeling helpless. She blew her nose and looked out the open window.

"What's the matter?" he finally asked.

She turned toward him, wiping her tears and biting her upper lip. "It's a dream I keep having," she said, the sparkle in her eyes returning. Nicholas knew that his excitement and tension, his attraction, even his awareness of her sadness all came together in that moment. He had that something-good-was-about-to-happen feeling.

"Why, is it a nightmare or something?"

"No, not really," she replied. "It's just this symbol I keep seeing. It's weird looking and it won't go away. I've been seeing it in my head everywhere I go."

"What does it look like," he asked.

"It's three concentric circles inside a triangle."

He nodded and gave her a blank look.

She slapped him lightly on the arm and said, "I bet you don't know what concentric circles are."

Flustered, he pursed his lips and squinted, searching for an answer that he knew he didn't have.

Lucy gave him the glimmer of a smile. "Here, I'll show you." She took out a red pencil from the cigar box beside him and carefully selected a sheet of blank paper from the inside of his binder notebook. Then she placed the paper on the floor and began to draw.

Without any hitch, she made three circles each one just inside the other, then drew a perfect triangle in the middle of them all. By the time she was done, Nicholas wanted to burst. "You mean you were crying because you saw that?" he asked in disbelief. She looked at him with such grave seriousness that it put him suddenly back into his place. "What is it?" he asked quietly, studying it really for the first time. Her lack of reply made him all the more curious.

He studied the symbol intensely, feeling quite odd as he did so. His head began to spin as it had the day his mom read the magazine to him. Everything in his room started to circle slowly about. He put both hands down beside him on the floor as if to hold on, trying to find a way to still his dizzy spell. Then he thought of the time he had flown with Tyco and centered all his attention on that same spot between his eyes, all the while feeling that he and Lucy were in a dream. They had done this before, somewhere, sometime ago or could it be the future?

The spinning room slowed down, then stopped altogether. Lucy came back into focus. The centering had worked. He could feel her watching him intently, any suspicion or doubt between them gone. Neither one of them had moved, not outwardly anyway, but he felt closer to her than he ever had with anyone on

Earth. She was like one of the little people, only right here sitting in his room, a flesh and blood creature, that he could even touch if he wanted.

"I only cried because I haven't had anyone to tell about this," Lucy said as she looked sadly at the symbol.

Nicholas wanted to help her. He knew as much as anyone how it felt to be so alone with such outlandish knowledge. "I'm sorry I was so stupid when you started crying," he said apologetically. "I didn't know how you felt."

Lucy brightened and put her hand on his shoulder. "Of course you didn't. I didn't either." They both looked at the symbol. "What do you think it means?

Nicholas felt the warmth of her hand as she placed it on his shoulder and knew that his face was flushed. Once again he controlled his mind and stilled his thoughts, staring into the center of the symbol. The three rings had to be special, three spheres of some kind maybe and the triangle defined them, gave them structure, a border of some sorts. The symbol could be a key, opening a doorway into another time and place.

His mind flowed into the symbol, Lucy's essence merging with his, searching for the answer together. He could feel Lucy and him and the symbol all merging, just as he saw in his mind's eye an image begin to form.

He closed his eyes then and relaxed. Two suns, one fiery red, and the other bright yellow shone down upon an aqua colored planet. It was the Land with Two Suns! As quick as recognition, he was whisked down to the bottom of the turquoise ocean. A group of silken amber creatures stood tall and regal beneath the water on a rocky plateau just outside the golden temple in the amazing white city.

He breathed in the ocean as if it were air, shocked that he could do so. The more he breathed, the more he let go of his fear that he might drown. No, nothing but pleasure followed as he realized he could not only survive, but feel quite comfortable in the alien environment. Letting go, that was the secret. One had to let go of fear in order to be secure. A message from one of the water beings in the crowd, transmitted by thought on waves of silence entered his mind. In a language so beautiful the message came, awakening his soul.

Tuapa mae rae oko sida
Kirien olamen tama ranen fala ken
tiernan fala ono
bisen ala kono
tiapa no raenen kala sen

Nicholas could feel the meaning behind the alien words, but not their exact translation, until the water being transferred that to him.

This place deep inside you
where lay memories of long ago
comes forward now
living once again
in the hearts and minds of those who listen

Nicholas felt alive with the spirit of the vision and the language. He wanted to keep the powerful words in his mind, but they started to drift away. Lucy took her hand away without a word and got up from the floor, then walked over to the window and looked out. "Did you see what I saw?" he asked excitedly.

"I saw a land with two suns," she replied matter of fact, "a red one and a yellow one, then it all faded."

"I saw it too," he said, jumping up and flapping his arms. "It has to be real!"

When she turned toward him and smiled, Nicholas decided to keep the rest of his vision to himself. If she didn't see anything more or if she didn't hear the alien language that was okay. He didn't want her to think that he was a know-it-all. No reason for it. Everyone was different. The fact that she saw the three spheres gave him a sense of relief. A planet with two suns didn't exactly fit into his science class description of Earth's solar system. No one on Earth had ever seen two suns close up like that.

Lucy was a charmer and a friend, someone he could rely on and trust. She could see like he did. That was important. Most of all, she was his friend.

"I heard something too," she said, turning on his radio on the table beside his bed, "something really beautiful that I keep hearing over and over."

"What's that?" he asked, sitting down on the bed.

"The sweet dreams beyond desire," she answered wistfully.

She flipped through the static filled stations one by one and finally settled on the rich sounds of some inspiring piano music. The song resonated in the small radio speaker. Then a woman on the radio began to sing along with the piano music.

Sweet dreams beyond desire,
Burn with passion in love's fire.

Nicholas and Lucy stared at each other dumbfounded, their eyes bugged from their heads and their mouths hanging open. The coincidence of Lucy's foreknowing had taken them both by surprise.

Lucy flipped through the stations again and settled on one. The exaggerated country and western drawl of a man singing a self-pitying honky-tonk song reverberated throughout the room. As the "wah wah" of a slide guitar cried in accompaniment to the man's singing, Lucy and Nicholas looked at each other and snickered. Lucy held onto the knob while they continued to listen.

Don't forget, dear, to think about me
When with that other man you will be.
We broke apart!
And now we'll start
Regretting our love lost
Just because,
Just because,
Because we can.

The song seemed so goofy to Nicholas. The man slurred the words with such a strong country accent that Nicholas could barely recognize some of them. Lucy started to cover her mouth with her hand, but burst out laughing. Her whole body shook with the uproarious tremor. Nicholas joined in the laughter, letting go with such force that he tossed about uncontrollably on the floor.

Lucy spun like a ballerina across the room, then back again, stretching up on her tip-toes, her whirling skirt rippling in a circle about her as she turned her long hair a blur of black around her face. As she danced back and forth to the comical music, Nicholas laughed so much that his stomach hurt, but when she slipped on the loose rug and landed with a thud on the hardwood floor, he lost what little was left of his composure. He lay on the floor helpless in a pool of his own giggles, with Lucy bent over him, poking him playfully in the ribs. The experience had unhinged him so, all because of Lucy. He would never forget this moment. Her friendship pleased him like no other.

They lay on their backs, panting for breath and trying to recover, their hands lightly touching. Nicholas knew then that he could trust Lucy.

"Would you like to make a dream pact?" he asked, his breath finally quieting down.

Lucy raised herself up and leaned on one elbow, staring into his eyes intently. Nicholas couldn't meet her gaze for very long. Although he trusted her, he didn't know for sure just how she would react to his suggestion. Lucy's chest heaved with exertion. Her black hair lay in curls about her face and the collar of her white blouse, accentuating her slender throat and the graceful curve where it met her jaw line.

"I wanted to ask you," he said staring at her jaw line, "because you seem to have the touch."

Feeling that Lucy must not understand his strange statement, he looked up at her. Her eyes questioned him as they narrowed with seriousness.

"You seem to know how dreams work," he added, feeling the odd sensation that though he shouldn't know that for a fact, Lucy understood that he did and accepted it.

Her lips widened slightly in the making of a smile that encouraged him. "Anyway, I've been dreaming about this little dwarf named Tyco that I'd like you to meet."

Lucy's smile grew; her eyes laughing in a way that he knew to be a good thing. She loved his confession.

"I figured that if we dreamed together we could meet up and get together with him. That is if he'll come. He's really old." Thinking of Tyco tickled Nicholas. He smiled at the prospect of dreaming with Lucy and added, "but Tyco's really lively."

Lucy shrugged her shoulders once and softly said, "sure."

Nicholas knew that when they slept that night on opposite sides of the street from at home in their beds a splendid adventure awaited them.

He would tell Lucy everything that had happened to him since he'd found the wondrous old hollow tree on the banks of the creek, but most importantly he'd ask her to make a dream pact. He knew that if they tried, they could dream together. Of all people, she would be able to find him in her dreams, and then they'd have an adventure to surpass anything before.

CHAPTER SIX

The dream pact held such mystery and excitement for Nicholas. Lucy had agreed whole-heartedly to the pact, a simple one really. They would meet in their dreams just after ten o'clock that night, as soon as they could go to sleep. In order to make sure it would happen they would both concentrate on Tyco's name, saying it over and over in their minds until they fell asleep.

Although Lucy had never seen Tyco, Nicholas had described him to her.

Nicholas had the strong feeling that the pact would work, especially after Lucy promised she would do her part with such conviction. He couldn't wait to go to sleep. Sometimes that prospect seemed so boring, but not this night.

He lay beneath the covers up to his chin, listening to the wind blowing through the elm tree outside his window. Sleeping could be fun, but it could be unpleasant too. Not all of his dreams were nice ones. Many times he had awakened in the middle of the night, scared out of his wits. Well, maybe not so many times, but it was hard to forget such nightmares, especially after he'd seen a really gruesome horror movie before going bed.

Dark shadows cast by moonlight played upon the wall, the stick figure people dancing in the wind, pantomiming each other to a rhythm that rocked him ever closer to sleep. He willed himself to relax, and convinced himself he must sleep as he closed his eyes to become the dreamer. The seconds ticked by on the clock beside him, his drifting awareness still conscious of the hour.

He had agreed to sleep at ten o'clock sharp and ten he knew it must be. Lucy had chosen the time earlier that day. Above all he must remember their dream pact, keep it uppermost in his mind. Lucy would be there, be there in his dreams.

As he dropped into slumber, a small part of him trusted that Lucy would remember their pact. Even as he dreamed, that trust stayed with him. Sometime before sunrise, he awoke only slightly, keenly aware that the dream pact was still unfulfilled. He fell back into sleep, with his intention clear and his purpose vivid. He had to find Lucy.

A cool fog touched him all over in his dream, the wetness like a blanket of sorrow surrounding him. There she was! He could see her now in a small clearing ahead. The fog parted more and more, revealing headstones all around that he passed as he walked toward her. It took a lot of effort to resist the urge to look at the names, the birth dates and death dates on each one. Something told him that what he was about to face would not be so easy.

Lucy stood alone, wearing a cloak of wool, the loose folds of its hood hanging across her face. He knew it was her though. She shook off the hood as he approached and looked down with great seriousness to a rectangular headstone in front of her. That would be his dead brother Ethan's marker. Again his intuition proved to be correct. Without surprise he read his brother's full name, Ethan Jules O'Malley, engraved upon the stone. This was too much. He didn't want to read the rest, but he forced himself to look at the inscription below.

Bring us closer, O' Lord,
to the sweet dreams beyond desire.

There it was again, that phrase that Lucy kept bringing to his attention. He'd completely forgotten that it had been etched onto Ethan's headstone. He hadn't wanted to remember. In fact he'd forgotten just how much he missed his brother.

One soulful look from Lucy and he wanted to cry. She understood his sadness. His love for Ethan left him weak with self-pity. His knees shook and he wanted to lie down, join Ethan in that sweet place beyond. He knew it was lovely there, like Lucy's face. He felt torn between two worlds. The past pulled upon him and weighed him down. If he could escape that, he'd be free, free to forget. Lucy put her arm around him and together they walked, slowly at first, then faster as he realized he had a companion and the lightening of his load made living more bearable. As their mood shifted rapidly and he managed to return Lucy's warmest of smiles, they began to skip. Lucy tossed off her cloak and with that one simple action, the landscape brightened.

That's when they saw Tyco, sitting on a big rock on the side of the path. The sight of the sprightly old dwarf tickled Nicholas. Lucy and the Ancient One stared at each other for a moment, the current of energy between them sparking off all around. Nicholas knew the two of them would get along.

Tyco hopped off the rock and stood firmly planted with a "What's next?" look on his face and his hands on his hips. When neither of the children did anything, he gave them a pouting sad face, turned about and walked bent over, pretending to be as stiff as he was old. Lucy and Nicholas followed close behind him, enjoying the sunshine and their comical leader.

At the approach to a large bridge of rusty old iron, Nicholas held Lucy's hand. Oh, the wonders of life! Sometimes it all seemed so grand. They walked out to the middle of the bridge and looked down. A strange but beautiful bubblegum pink stream flowed quietly beneath them. How could it be?

He had never seen such a thing before. Then he remembered he was dreaming and smiled inwardly. Anything was possible here. Lucy pointed at a long blue fish shooting up out of the stream and landing with a smack on its side in the thick liquid.

41

Another fish popped up out of the stream, then another and another, each one ejected up with a suction popping sound, until dozens of them arced over it in schools, slicing the air with their tall spiny back fins and landing with a baloop or a plop.

The dream felt so rich to Nicholas. The more it continued, the more he knew that he would be okay. He found it easy to gather his thoughts and easier to enjoy the moment. Tyco and Lucy were his best friends in the world and he could finally relax, at least a little. There would be new experiences and hard times to try his patience, but he would cherish them too, knowing in his heart that he was no longer alone.

The beauty and the magic of the land engulfed him as he stepped into Tyco's footsteps. They lay in a long row before him, the sunken boot tracks in the soft soil matching his sneakers.

Tyco started hopping with his hands and feet close together like bunny paws. Lucy smiled at Nicholas, giggling, and then dropped his hand. She ran after Tyco and walked by his side. She too was quite a bit taller than the dwarf.

Tyco twitched his nose and sniffed her as any rabbit might do, then sat down on his haunches. Lucy leaned down and petted him happily. He took it quite well, crooning and enjoying the affection, but suddenly he jumped up and toppled forward in a delightful series of somersaults. They both ran along beside him, patting and pushing him forward occasionally with their hands. To their surprise and amazement, Tyco had transformed himself. In his place crawling about on the beet red grass were hundreds of long squiggly blue worms. They came together, squeaking loudly as they did so, braiding themselves in a thick rope that tied itself together end to end in a big circle like a hoop. The worm hoop rolled forward and careened down the hill in front of them. The children screeched with laughter and merriment. They skipped and jumped, then somersaulted too, rolling down the hill after the worms.

Nicholas sat at the bottom of the hill and noticed his hands and his clothes as well as Lucy's were all covered with a bright red liquid. "Look, Lucy," he said pointing at her hands, "there's blood all over you."

Lucy, who stood tall beside him, glanced at her red-stained fingers and gasped. She looked down at the hem of her pleated skirt and started to shake. Nicholas noticed that the hillsides around them were covered with thick short grasses a deep beet red color.

"It's not blood," Nicholas said confidently with a smile, his palms held open and his arms stretched out toward the hillside. "It's just grass stains. The grass is red here; that's all."

Lucy looked about and immediately stopped shaking. "Aiyee," she screeched with relief, wiping her hands on her skirt. She sat down beside Nicholas on the grass, put her elbows up on her upraised knees and rested her chin there.

"Isn't this a strange place?" Nicholas commented as the bright blue worm rope rolled down the hill past them. It continued to roll farther, losing its momentum, then falling over on its side in the grass, whirling about, each gyration growing smaller and smaller, until it finally stopped. The worms unbraided themselves and crawled silently down into the sticky red grass where they disappeared. Tyco had left them.

"I wonder where Tyco is going," Nicholas said. "Isn't he great?"

"Hard to tell," Lucy said.

"Don't you just love it here?" Nicholas asked as he looked at the sky.

Dark clouds moved in, building up all around them. Suddenly he felt the mood had shifted. Tyco had left them and he didn't feel nearly as brave as he had.

Lucy looked at her hands again as if that would tell her how to answer. She too began to look worried. "Yeah, it's great."

The wind started to blow, a cold force of nature that chilled them. Nicholas felt a twinge of fear that grew as Tyco didn't return and the wind menaced them, blowing dust in their eyes and grit into their teeth. What had happened to Tyco? Maybe he wasn't coming back and they would be alone to figure out what to do next by themselves. That might have been all right, but why couldn't Tyco have stayed?

The temperature dropped and Lucy snuggled up to Nicholas for comfort. Bad things usually happened at times like this, just when he was having so much fun too. How would they ever find their way around? He decided that walking would be better than staying still, better to keep them warm. They got up together without a word. Oh man, Tyco was a jerk!

A flock of large black birds circled above them. "Those birds don't look too friendly," Nicholas said, trying to sound calmer than he was. He put his arm around Lucy's shoulders as they hunkered down. Maybe the birds wouldn't see them.

"Oh Nicholas," Lucy said, shivering beside him. "What are we going to do?"

Nicholas could actually hear Lucy's teeth rattle, which made him start to shiver as well... the cold and the wind and now these birds! The birds heavy wings made ominous booming sounds with every flap, vibrating the very ground beneath them. Nicholas almost picked Lucy up with him as he stood. They had to do something. The birds flew lower and lower, until Nicholas could see their long beaks and menacing sharp talons. Lucy and he could be killed!

The birds swooped down at the children, diving at great speed straight for them, snapping their beaks and baring long jagged teeth. The birds' ominous yellow eyes oozed masses of puke green puss that rained down upon the children. The puss seared the children with a heat so fierce, as it landed upon their exposed skin that they both screamed out in holy terror.

The children started to run hand in hand, ducking and dodging the birds the best they could. One bird, larger than all the rest, came at Nicholas with such grotesque fierceness. It pecked at his arm as he raised it to protect himself. He thought he would die from fear alone. The bird grabbed at his forearm with its razor-sharp beak and tore a bite from his flesh that made him scream. He almost dragged Lucy as he ran even faster, going nowhere in particular, just running for his life. They had to find shelter.

Bad turned to worst. The birds landed all around them, a solid frightening mob, and a bloodthirsty circle wishing the children's death.

Nicholas could hardly breathe and definitely couldn't speak. He froze in that instant, afraid of his fear, with Lucy beside him just as helpless. The fearless birds walked slowly, but steadily toward the children on long scaled wiry legs. Their huge talons tore at the grass, squeezing it with blood lust as they bore down upon their prey, closing the circle and tightening the noose. The birds had them every way that Nicholas could imagine.

Nicholas gulped with great relief as Tyco suddenly appeared beside him, raising his small but mighty hands for a moment in silence, his face impassive and powerful, a look of complete control upon it.

"Tahla," the Ancient One shouted out, shaking his hands at the birds. "Inbix tulah," he added with such force that his incantation pushed them back from the shock wave.

The birds all took off at once, their flapping wings blowing the dream seekers all about. Unruffled, Tyco looked at Nicholas and Lucy both as if nothing had happened, but they crowded in close to him for safety as the birds flew off in the distance and the sun came out from behind the clouds.

"You'll have to be careful what you think if you want to stay here," Tyco said. "It is a hard lesson, but you must know that I would have returned to you eventually. You could have created something more pleasant for yourself, but instead you chose to give in to your fear which attracted the birds."

Tyco put one hand on Lucy and one on Nicholas and closed his eyes. The children's scratches and Nicholas' wound immediately healed before their eyes and disappeared. It was almost like the birds hadn't even come down on them. Nicholas' relief embarrassed him. He knew now that he had created the situation with the birds. Well, maybe Lucy had helped. She looked at him with a sense of wonder on her face. This was a different kind of place.

Tyco skipped off then, and they had to run to catch up. Rolling purple hills covered with tall purple plants that swayed in the breeze like palm trees stretched off to the horizon as far as Nicholas could see in all directions. The beauty of the purple place made Nicholas ache with an energy that not only lifted his spirits, but also made him run fastest of all. He took off, passing Tyco, galloping for all that he was worth, feeling then that no other experience had ever made him feel so free. His heart beat and his breath heaved, but he didn't care. He felt that he could gallop all day at full speed like a racehorse.

Something about the land had captured his fancy. This place could be so great if only he could show it to people when he was awake. His mother and his father would appreciate it just as much as he, if only they could see it. His friends at school, his teacher Mrs. Morrison, everyone would find the place divine. God must live here. That was that. He had decided. This was where God lived. Pleased with himself, he stopped. Just then, Lucy and Tyco appeared by his side.

"Oberron is my homeland," Tyco said. "Although it is not always friendly it is the best of places to live. Your thoughts can turn against you here very quickly. Everyone knows that of course, so we are extra careful what we think."

That seemed understandable as Nicholas knew it correct first hand. He had turned the birds against himself and Lucy by simply thinking bad thoughts. No, he wouldn't do that again anytime in the near future.

"Your world is not so unlike ours," Tyco explained further. "Some things change a little bit faster and are more obvious here, but the basics are the same." With a fatherly expression, he looked first at Lucy then at Nicholas who walked on each side of him.

No sooner had he said this than a monkey appeared in Lucy's arms. "See what I mean?" Tyco said smiling and giving the monkey a pat. "Lucy thought about friendship and this furry little creature instantly appeared."

Tyco made a sweeping gesture at the hills around them. "Dreams and memories are the money of Oberron. We hold these things precious above all else and use them to trade for everything we need. We call your world Emkhoura and have deep memories of it that go far back to the most ancient of times. Once we lived there too and walked freely about, but now it is too harsh for us."

"I'm afraid Emkhoura is sick," Tyco said, looking solemn. "We only visit there in our dreams to sing the two worlds together. Otherwise, they would drift completely apart." Tyco stuck his hands in his pockets and frowned mournfully at the ground. "If that happens," he croaked, "our planet will die. Oberron is the soul while Emkhoura is the body. They both need each other, though most humans don't know that it's true. Sometime you will see us if you try hard enough. Look for us dwarves in the field or by the stream at twilight on the full moon."

Their pace quickened with their longing to see more of Oberron. The road took them down further and further into the heart of a luscious blue valley.

Icicles started growing on Nicholas' chin. The blue color of the mountains on either side of them had made him think of winter. Though the lovely peaks stood tall, their small troupe of adventurers walked in a low lush valley with tropical looking plants all about them.

Snow began to fall then, but for the life of him, Nicholas couldn't figure out from where, as the sky looked as cloudless and bright as ever. The large round flakes like wafers melted on his face and arms though he sweated beneath his t-shirt. Nothing about the day seemed cold at all now. Lucy too looked warm, her face flush as if she had walked for miles. How long had they been walking? He couldn't be sure of time at all, but then it didn't really matter.

The monkey sat proudly on Lucy's shoulder like a little soldier with his pointed red hat and button down uniform. He jumped over Tyco's head and landed on Nicholas' shoulder, then reached out and plucked a dagger shaped icicle and popped one end in his tiny mouth. That did it. Nicholas realized that he had created the winter effect around them. Immediately, it stopped snowing.

He enjoyed knowing how thoughts could make events happen. Funny how in the old days before meeting Tyco, he hadn't noticed that his thoughts effected his environment nearly so much. The dream pact had been a good idea. He and Lucy had learned something that they could use when they went back to Emkhoura. Emkhoura, he liked the sound of the name. It sounded like an ancient and splendid place, a grand name for Earth. Emkhoura could be a fun place, though it had certainly been difficult a lot of the time too.

The monkey began to poke around in Nicholas' hair, searching for fleas, chattering noisily in his ear as he did so. Of course monkeys had to be monkeys, as people had to be people, but what were dwarves really like? He had less experience with their kind than most. Tyco walked without a care in the world, his head held high, enjoying the day. His eyes shone as he looked at something up ahead.

The small village that they came to had a fascinating quality about it, like a toy town only bigger. The houses looked clean and well-built the rooftops smooth and black like slabs of licorice with smoking red chimneys that actually coughed in the funniest way. Coughing chimneys, who would have thought he'd ever see one? The chimney bricks of each one flew apart every time that one coughed, then fell back together in place, sending up small puffs of black smoke as it did so.

All around the village, the coughing chimneys belched and burped in a comical code that seemed like conversation, though he couldn't understand what they said. The streets were made of some kind of hay, golden shafts of crisp material that crinkled as Nicholas walked upon it. Many dwarves of all sizes and ages hurried hither and thither, going about what looked like all kinds of important business.

Tyco stopped to chat with one of the local lady dwarves who stood in her yard clipping the hedge, or more accurately, watching the clippers trim the hedge. Suspended in the air, the clippers clipped away on their own while she supervised with her arms crossed on her chest, nodding at this cut and that.

As she moved her head from side to side appraising the angles of the hedge, large brown nutshells that dangled from the braids of her long black hair whistled in the breeze. Her rosy cheeks and chubby figure made her look like the most friendly of dwarves. Her dress made of a woven silver material glinted in the sunlight. To Nicholas' great surprise, when she turned side-ways, she disappeared altogether. Then she appeared again, the nuts in her hair dangling and whistling their approval. Nicholas was getting used to people disappearing and reappearing, though he hadn't done it himself yet.

"Tuatha dey lanen bena mensen kala fen," the dwarf lady said, bending her head toward Lucy and Nicholas.

Tyco nodded knowingly, while he too watched the clippers clipping away with a snip-snip.

The lady's words surprised Nicholas at first and gave him a tingling sensation in his stomach and chest. The queasy sensation didn't hurt, but he wanted to shake off the discomfort. He wasn't sure, but he had the feeling that the lady spoke of Lucy and him, that somehow she knew why they were there in Oberron and understood their purpose. Nicholas wished more than anything that he understood that purpose as well.

Other dwarves started to gather about them, watching the clippers in their magical motion and listening as the nuts on the lady's dress whistled in the breeze. Nicholas looked at Lucy standing beside him near the hedge to see if she had understood the dwarf lady's words. Lucy seemed just as puzzled as he did. Then he recalled that on the land with two suns, the silken creature at the bottom of the turquoise ocean had spoken to him in such a language. Lucy had been with him that day as well. He tuned into the dwarf lady and Tyco, letting Tyco's response to her flow over him. Nicholas' need to know made him pay ever-closer attention, until the meaning of the words rang clear in his mind.

"They come from Emkhoura to visit our fair land," Tyco said. "Let me introduce you to them."

Nicholas knew that had Tyco had spoken in the strange foreign language. He also knew that Lucy and he were dreaming about the land of Oberron. The fact that he could understand the dwarves' language made him feel as if he were dreaming within the dream, doing the impossible. The boundaries of his mind were stretching far beyond their normal range and he loved it.

Even as Tyco introduced Lucy and himself to the dwarf lady of the hedge, he felt that his mind was stretching even farther than before. He knew that he heard Tyco introduce him and Lucy in the dwarf language and understood every bit of it, but he didn't listen anymore to the words. Euphoria came over him, a welcome and gratifying sensation that made him feel weightless, timeless, without a body in fact. He no longer felt that he owned his body or that he even had one. His spirit knew freedom for that short time. Then he came back into the conversation, hearing the dwarf ladies' gentle words as she looked him squarely in the eyes and spoke melodically to him. "Are you ready for the change?" the lady asked.

The lady's words baffled Nicholas and sent his mind instantly spinning with confusion. Just what change did she speak of? The words of Tyco's song came back to him. "We have returned to this hour, to rekindle the flame of nature's power. That power that grows each passing day will crack the stone and awake the clay." The change must have something to do with an Earth change, something big beyond the power of humankind. That thought gave him a little confidence, though he feared his part in the change might mean more than he understood. He tried to show only composure. "I only hope so," he answered.

He knew that the lady could see through him. Her warm eyes made him feel comfortable once again, as if she had the power of the Earth emanating from within them. That power radiated from her as she spoke. "The Earth will change and Emkhoura will be cleansed. The people of Oberron wish it to be so." The lady stood with her hands clasped, palms upward as if she carried the weight of the Earth's burden in them. She looked at Lucy then as she spoke. "Though the Earth will shake and spew forth new blood to cleanse herself, she will not harm those who hold nature's law close to their hearts."

The lady's rosy cheeks glowed bright red and Nicholas felt the fire within her embrace him. He felt warmed by her as if she now carried the power of the sun to give life. Her eyes twinkled with love

"Both of you must learn about yourselves first, and then you will find your place in Emkhoura."

Feeling the presence of the others behind him, Nicholas turned around and found to his delight that the crowd of dwarves had grown quite large. There was the little boy dressed in crimson who had played the drum in his other dream. When the boy came forward from the crowd and saw Nicholas, his blonde hair curled up on the ends. The boy's enchanting smile lit a flame in Nicholas' heart. His small hands fidgeted with an uncontainable nervous energy. Like a flash, he pulled forward the small drum he had slung about his back on a cord and began to play. The boy's hands moved so fast with precision and energy. Nicholas took Lucy's hand and got down on one knee, watching every move the boy made. The boy's tapping out of the rapid and moving rhythm made Lucy tightly squeeze his hand, her pulse beating in time with it.

The rest of the group started to dance to the beat of the little boy's drum. Hundreds of tiny silver bells attached to their clothing jingled in wave after wave of delightful sound as the dwarves stomped their feet and moved their arms in the most fascinating way.

The eerie and outlandish music gave Nicholas goose bumps. This group was truly alive! They moved about each other, turning and circling in a wheel. Lucy and Nicholas stood in the center enraptured and enthralled. Oberron was such a wonderful place! The dwarves slapped their knees and their bellies and each other lightly with the beat, singing in hushed tones which only made their words all the more intense.

Relax, relax
And you will see
The life that you can weave.

Perhaps, perhaps
Then you'll be free
To plant the magic seed.

To grow, to grow
Go to and fro
Until the plan you'll know.

Rebirth, rebirth
Come touch the earth
Let sadness go and feel the mirth.

But Nicholas did feel sad, just as he had in the caverns of his first dream with Tyco. The pain that surged in his chest threatened to overtake him. He choked, but unlike the chimneystacks coughing up smoke on the rooftops around them, he couldn't get the feeling out. He feared that he would die if he didn't do something. He knew what the sadness was, knew that he felt the pain of the Earth, the way people treated each other and neglected and abused the Earth. Even the animals, the plants, all the kingdoms of the world, all the species and types, from the highest to the lowest mineral all felt that neglect and discord.

Oh sure, people could laugh and enjoy themselves for a while, but he knew it was often short lived and the dreaded aftermath of their sorrow a heaviness that wouldn't go away. He knew that it was so, even though he also knew that many people ignored their pain, unable to change it. The suffering had him too. The song had only brought it to the surface. Lucy stood beside him looking gloomy. Evidently the song had affected her in a similar way.

The lady stepped through her hedge as if it wasn't there and stood in front of Nicholas and Lucy. She took Nicholas' hand in hers and said, "My name is Lenora. Please, let us share memories." She looked at Nicholas, a deep look that told him there was nothing to hide.

He closed his eyes and concentrated. A memory came to him immediately of Lucy drawing the strange symbol that day at his house. The three rings about the triangle that she drew gave him the vision of the land with two suns, one orange and one red. The memories passed from himself to Lenora, through his hands and easily into hers. He felt that he was actually giving Lenora something very special and valuable. Lenora also received the memory that he projected to her of the gold and silver temple. It radiated light from the center of the beautiful white city at the bottom of the turquoise ocean. The memory of Lucy and himself rolling on the floor also passed from himself to her, just before her memories started coming into his own mind.

Lenora gave him an image of a beautiful turquoise stone of a sky blue color that lay in her palm. In his mind's eye, he saw her hand it to him. He too received the gift with an open heart, feeling blessed by the trade and opportunity to share something so dear to both of them. Lenora let go of his hands then. With his eyes open, he scanned the crowd now standing in a circle about Lucy, Lenora, and him.

The dwarves stood silent. Slowly like a dream, each one put his arms around the back of the person next to him or her. Their solemn looks made Nicholas uncomfortable. He couldn't look at them anymore. Perhaps they expected him to do something for the Earth. The grief that he felt for the Earth was still there, though sharing memories had eased it some. Sadness could be like that. So often you couldn't even tell where it came from or why it came. He did feel the anguish of the Earth and people and all life, but how was he supposed to live in the way that he knew he could? The joy deep inside him kept getting stepped on. There must be other people that felt as he did, but no one spoke out for the Earth and all of her children. Maybe they weren't strong enough. He had to find a way to speak without scaring everyone so much.

Lucy cared about the Earth and people. He could feel that. The warmth of her hand told him so. The dwarves in the circle around him cared. He could see that in their eyes, but his sadness stayed. There were just too many people that suffered even more than he did. He knew that life could be wonderful. Maybe his pain wasn't even his. Maybe it was everybody's, like a shared lesson that one had to reckon with. Could that be it?

He looked up into the eyes of the dwarves around him. A hint of light there grew as he scanned around the circle. Yes, they must feel as he did about life.

"Though the path is hard, your friends are with you," the little boy said standing before Nicholas, looking as sincere as one could. "We too know the sufferings of the Earth," he continued, "but together we can make a difference."

If a small child could put such a complex idea into simple terms, then Nicholas could go on. Nothing about the boy could be mistaken. He was what you saw, a gift of nature. It was silly for Nicholas to flounder in sorrow like a boy without a home. Nicholas' questioning of life could get too heavy, too much to bear. All he had to do was release the sadness and share, just like in the dwarves' song. The boy looked openly at him, waiting.

The crowd opened up, letting Lucy's monkey in. It scampered over to the little boy and jumped up into his arms. At this signal, everyone looked up. A tall slender lady with dark long tresses wearing a long golden gown stepped forward barefoot through the crowd. In her hands before her, she reverently held a silver serving tray that sparkled in the sun. She stopped in front of the little blonde haired boy and offered him the tray. He picked out a green peanut shaped morsel from others of many colors and stuffed it in his mouth.

As he chewed noisily and looked from Lucy to Nicholas, the light in his eyes grew brighter and they turned from jet black to electric blue.

The fine lady curtsied before Lucy, one hand holding out the hem of her dress to the side and the other offering her the tray. With only a little hesitation, Lucy selected one of the largest orange-colored peanuts and took a small bite.

Surprised that Lucy's choice of food had no noticeable effect upon her, Nicholas felt a small let down, but when the lady offered him the tray with her head bent downward and arms extended, he felt like royalty with so many colors to choose from. He picked out a blue peanut-shaped piece and bit into it, half expecting his nose to twitch or something even stranger to happen.

At first, the most succulent of mint tastes cooled his senses. Then those tastes suddenly exploded in his mouth like seven thousand bolts of lightning, making him laugh crazily with joy and relief.

CHAPTER SEVEN

Nicholas woke up laughing out loud, something he didn't usually do. The food the beautiful lady had given him had tasted like laughter. That idea seemed odd, food that tasted like laughter. It felt like some kind of medicine, changing his insides from dark to light. The little people made him happy, though he had encountered many darker parts of himself in the dream. All in all, he felt good. Waking up laughing made him optimistic. God, that was scary. How long would it last? No telling just when the next blast of trouble would come. There it was, the enemy, pessimism. Pessimism was a fun word. Pessimism, pessimism, no, trouble didn't have quite the scare that it used to. The little people had taken out some of that sting. Tyco had showed him how to control his thoughts to create a better life. That's what he would do, be ever vigilant, watch and monitor his thoughts. He would succeed even if he slipped.

The loud knock at his door jolted him out of his thoughts. That was probably Lucy; at least he hoped it was. She would want to talk about the dream. Before he could open the door, she flew in and caught him frozen mid-stride on the floor, wearing nothing but his underwear. He freaked. Oh well, she would have to handle it. His mother must be slipping. It wasn't like her to let people into his room before he even got out of bed.

Lucy scanned him up and down, surprised. He grabbed his shirt and his pants off the chair and opened the closet door. That would be the only safe place to dress. He felt silly and stupid in the closet once he closed the door and switched on the light. He hadn't even said hello or anything, but then who knew that she would barge in to his room? She had seen him half naked.

"I'll be out in a minute," he yelled struggling with his pant leg. It took him several tries, but he finally managed to get one foot through.

"Nicholas, I saw you in my dream last night," Lucy yelled back at him, "you and Tyco both." It was clear that she was excited, but how had she known Tyco by his name? Stranger things had happened. The dreams were making them both psychic. He was just glad that she remembered her dream. Not many people could do that. He knew, because he had lots of dreams with people, but when he asked them if they remembered what had happened the next day, they looked at him as if he were a giant lobster or something.

Lucy was sitting on his bed when he opened the door, almost fully dressed. He sat down beside her to put on his sneakers, feeling her closeness though she didn't seem to be paying much attention to it. "What did Tyco mean, Nicholas?" Lucy asked puzzled. "He said I would see you again one day after you left?" Her disheveled hair only made her look more wild and beautiful than ever.

Nicholas shrugged his shoulders, sidetracked. This girl had charm that hadn't been invented yet. She grabbed him by the shoulder and shook him.

"What do you mean?" she said exasperated. "He said you were going to leave."

It was all Nicholas could do to concentrate. The whole series of events, from the dream the night before to her uninvited, but not altogether disagreeable intrusion had him in a state. He wanted to laugh, but that seemed inappropriate.

"I don't remember anything about Tyco saying I was going anywhere," he said pleased with his comeback.

"Oh Jeez," Lucy said, getting up and storming out of the room.

Nicholas just sat there stunned, listening to her footsteps as she bounced down the stairs. Evidently he had upset her, but his confusion had him spinning. What was going on?

Later that day, Nicholas finally found Lucy, sitting on the curb in front of her house as if waiting for him. She didn't seem too friendly when he came up to her and sat down though. She wouldn't even look at him. Girls could truly be difficult. Maybe he was just stupid.

He sat down beside her with his hands clenched before him, inspecting a thin line of red ants running pell-mell back to their big anthill that they were building a few feet away. It was fascinating how they could follow each other carrying such heavy loads, huge boulders of sand weighing as much as seven times their own weight.

He felt ill at ease and incapable. What was he supposed to do anyway? Girls always seemed to know more than guys. It was as if they were magicians, but they didn't know it. They just took their knowledge for granted and expected guys to know more than they did. Nicholas did know that Lucy had become extremely outraged because he was leaving. He wouldn't want to leave. Lucy and he had become such good friends almost overnight, at least he thought they were.

She cleared her throat and glanced at him, tears streaming down her face. Oh boy, that was something that always got to him. He had hurt her feelings. He just knew that he had.

"I didn't mean to hurt your feelings," he apologized. With a stick, she drew lines in the dust in the gutter, then scratched them all out and jumped up.

When she took off running like a streak down the street, her long black hair trailing behind her, Nicholas jumped up too. He wasn't letting her get away this time. He had to catch her.

That was no easy task. She had a couple years on him and her legs were actually longer than his, but he did catch her, using all

59

of his speed and every bit of effort. When he caught up to her, she just stopped, right there in the middle of the street, the wind blowing both of them angrily about. Nicholas felt angry too, but he didn't know why. It wasn't Lucy's fault. He just felt that something powerful and out of his control had stepped into his life. There was a larger plan that they had uncovered and he still didn't quite understand.

They started walking together at the same time then as if someone had told them to. They walked slowly, entranced, the mood overtaking them as the wind rose up above and whipped the elm trees high overhead. It was funny how the wind could move about like that. It seemed to talk to them, a special message that he imagined he could almost understand. There weren't any words. The wind didn't speak in words. It spoke more in feelings and he felt them in his heart. Lucy and he were meant to be together. That's what the wind was trying to help them feel. It was talking to them. He didn't feel angry now, just thankful and grateful. This girl and he had a connection that went beyond words and howdy do's. They had an understanding.

That night Nicholas found out what Tyco had meant when he told Lucy that she would see Nicholas again one day after he left. His mother told him with hardly any expression on her face, that their family was moving to Colorado, because his father had a big job to do there and for that reason it was a better place to live. Nicholas was crushed. The thought of leaving made him half sick. More than anything or anyone, he would miss Lucy. Without her he'd be alone again.

He lay soberly on his bed, turning his prospects over and over in his head when he heard heavy footsteps coming up the stairs. That was his father. He dreaded the encounter. His father could be such a pain. When his father knocked, he jumped up from the bed as if pulled by puppet strings and opened the door.

His father had a familiar devilish look on his face. He stood there as tall as a skyscraper and just as solid, a powerful man; muscular and tanned, wearing white cotton plastering clothes, holding a tall glass full of some alcoholic concoction. Small pieces of dried plaster still hung from the curls of his thick black hair and heavy eyebrows, a sure sign and not a good one that he hadn't taken his shower or eaten yet. His mood could be horrible under those conditions.

"What's up, kiddo?" his dad said, swirling his glass that clinked with ice cubes as he strode into the room. His father looked about the white and blue plastered walls and ceiling, admiring his work and set the drink down on Nicholas's desk.

"Not much," Nicholas said, putting his hands in his pockets wand sitting down on the bed, wanting to be invisible. These little conversations of theirs were not his favorite. His father usually went away with Nicholas feeling trapped. Most of the time his father just wanted Nicholas to do some chore or another and bargained with Nicholas by seeming to take interest in his life. Not that Nicholas had any real choice. He always had to do what his father said or else. He didn't even bother finding out what punishment might be like, not anymore. His father was so frightening that Nicholas couldn't imagine not obeying his father. Tonight was different though. Nicholas hadn't done anything wrong. Now that they were leaving town, his father would probably talk about that.

"You always wanted to live on top a mountain, didn't you?" his father asked without looking at him.

Nicholas shrugged his shoulders and feigned a laugh, too nervous to be honest. This was the ultimate challenge. In this position, time stood still and every word flew like an arrow into his heart. He didn't want to move away. He summoned up his courage, remembering Tyco's advice to not let his fears rule him. His pessimism could make his life worse. He knew it. Now was his chance.

For a moment, he felt that a balance had been struck between him and his father. Monitoring his thoughts instead of giving in to them completely had given him hope. There must be some reason too that Tyco had told Lucy that she'd see him again. Maybe something good would come of the move after all. He had to find the bright side.

"It would be good," Nicholas said, trying to believe it. The mountains had always intrigued him ever since he could remember. The huge rocks at the rooftop of the world had an appeal he couldn't find where they lived now, which was fairly flat, mostly prairie and low elevation. Though he loved the creek and the sand hills outside of town, Colorado did sound good. What adventures he could have. Maybe Lucy could come to visit. That thought embarrassed him, thinking that his father might read his mind. People did that sometimes without even knowing what they were doing. He wouldn't feel comfortable telling his father about Lucy. That was his secret.

It was hard to believe that his thoughts had shifted so quickly. Only moments before, he had been depressed about leaving Kansas. Now he found himself going along with the program and not resenting it completely. Having inside information could be handy in times like this, so could self-understanding. Even so he had to be careful with his father. He was the kind of guy that could blow up at any minute without warning.

"Anyway, we won't be moving for a while," his father said cheerily. "Why don't you and I go fishing tonight?" That was a first. Nicholas had never been fishing all night with his dad, though he knew that was one of his dad's favorite activities.

"All right," he answered.

Encouraged, his father slapped him on the knee, and then backed up in a boxing stance like a prizefighter, his eyes bulging with good humor. "Yeah, we'll break out the boat and show those fish a thing or two," his father added, punching at the air in front of him.

Nicholas smiled at his father. Sometimes his father could be a blast.

The fishing trip that evening turned out much different than Nicholas expected. He never knew just how events would turn out with his father. There was always a surprise waiting somewhere.

They arrived at the Big Muddy River about 60 miles from home at around ten o'clock. His mother hadn't given him any flack about going, though she knew they would probably be out all night. He usually had to go to bed by at least midnight on the weekend. But then life had changed for Nicholas. He was getting older. Fishing in the middle of the night sounded so mysterious. He'd never even been awake all night at home, not to mention out on the river in the middle of nowhere where anything could happen.

As they glided up the river in their aluminum boat, his father rowing capably at the stern like some Viking sailor, Nicholas felt like they were going back in time. The trees formed a dark arch overhead that blotted out the moon, making the light faint and his senses more alert. Behind them in the distance, he heard the muffled boom of thunderclaps. A storm brewed. The humid air hung close, hugging the murky water and filling his lungs with promise.

"Take that line and tie it to the side," his father instructed.

Nicholas did as he was told, tying the nylon cord of the fish stringer in a double knot on the railing of the boat. This was too good to be true. He turned up the kerosene lantern sitting on the bottom of the boat and looked at his father. Usually he asked first to do such a thing, but tonight was different. His father and he were almost equals now. Their adventure made it so.

"Do you think they'll be biting tonight?" he asked enthused.

His father slowly pulled one more time upon the oars before answering. "This is the best time to catch something. They love this kind of weather."

Nicholas knew what to do after his dad told him only once, instructing him in the art of bank line fishing.

They didn't talk much for quite a while. He loaded the lines with stink bait, the most awful smelling stuff in the universe. It came in a jar, thick and gooey brown stuff that made him gag every time he pulled some out with his fingers, but he didn't care. After a while, baiting the hooks got to be fun. Nicholas' dad would row them to the next likely spot that he thought would be a good place to catch a fish and Nicholas would portion out the bait on the hooks. Then Nicholas would jab the bank line stick into the mud, in the weeds or the underside of a rock. Over and over they did this, going back and forth from one side of the river to the other, setting out bank lines, until they ran out of sticks.

It was funny to imagine they might catch fish without even watching or holding their pole. He'd never tried it before, but his father acted as if he had done it a thousand times. Every move he made was smooth and calculated like a professional, his knowledge of the river beyond anyone's Nicholas had ever known.

The rustling of brush nearby on the bank startled Nicholas. He held the light up to get a look. Two tiny lights close together, that he knew to be eyes, reflected back from the weeds, then were gone. It must have been a coon or a badger, something that liked to move about in the dark.

Nicholas' father and he rowed their boat back down the river and returned to their starting spot. Nicholas checked their first bank line, which had a decent sized catfish struggling upon it. He pulled it into the boat and in his eagerness to display it for his father, carelessly picked it up by the head. It jabbed him not only once, but twice in a flash with a bony fin as sharp as a sword, slicing the side of his thumb with a terrible pain.

"Aahh," he exhaled between clenched teeth as he dropped the fish into the bottom of the boat. He glanced at his dad, half expecting a reprimand, then back at his bloody thumb. His dad had told him many times to never pick up a catfish that way

His father took out a big white handkerchief from the front pocket of his khaki pants as a bullfrog croaked several times from the bank and the wind suddenly began to blow. The storm would be upon them soon. "Here, let's wrap this around it," his dad said, twirling the handkerchief up into a thick band and applied it to the wound. "That's a nasty cut. Those catfish can be mean."

His father's lack of anger pleased Nicholas. It wasn't too often that his dad showed his gentle side. Just about any little thing usually set him off. The bullfrog croaked again several times as if filling in the awkward space. Nicholas didn't know what to say. By his father's silence, he assumed that he had accepted Nicholas' mistake. Nicholas and his father could say more without words than with them. They understood each other at that moment.

There was no need for judgment or ridicule. It was enough to just be together.

As the fish on their stringer multiplied, Nicholas found himself thinking how primitive the catfish looked swimming beside the boat in the lantern light. Their whiskers intrigued him, long black tendrils that looked like handle bar mustaches on old western gunslingers. That's probably why they called them catfish, because of their whiskers.

"What are their whiskers for?" Nicholas asked nonchalantly.

"They can actually smell with them," his father replied, pushing off from the bank and picking up the oars. "Catfish are tough. They're about the hardest thing to kill." It began to rain lightly, blotching Nicholas and his father's clothes and making everything slick.

His father's answer perplexed Nicholas. How could they smell with their whiskers? He knew better than to quiz too much.

"I've been stung by catfish a few times myself," his father said extending his fist and displaying several wicked scars on the backs of his knuckles.

Nicholas leaned over and looked at them in awe, his pain disappearing at the sight of his father's gnarled hand. "Wow, that must have hurt!"

His father laughed as if proud of himself. "I'm just kidding. That happened when I got caught in the thrasher belt on the combine."

"Oh, God," Nicholas said. "Man that really must have hurt." He didn't know what to make of their newfound camaraderie. He was so used to being badgered by his father that he found the moment a mixture of pleasantness and discomfort.

The rest of their bank lines provided them with more catfish, a couple flathead and of course too many carp, which they tossed, still living and quite full of life, back into the river.

It wasn't until they reached their last bank line that something really strange happened. Nicholas had stuck the last bank line back in a dark pocket near the base of a fallen locust tree lying on the bank. It looked like a witches' lair, the tangled roots and cobwebs like hair, the mud slippery and wet.

His father did the honors, putting down the oars and reaching for the stick. He pulled it out easily enough from the sucking mud and raised it high. Lightning split the air over their heads with a crack, and they both jumped as the flash illuminated a long black snake, hissing and writhing about on the hook, its red tongue darting in and out of its gaping mouth. His father, face stricken white with horror, dropped the snake back into the water. He sat hunched up in the boat like a scared child, shaking.

"Did you see that?" his father asked, seeking sympathy. Nicholas nodded his head yes, feeling a great disappointment. He'd never seen his dad so frightened, truly frightened. Sure, the lightning flash and the sudden appearance of such an unexpected catch had startled them both, but he knew as much as his dad that bull snakes weren't poisonous. Of course his dad had been a lot closer to it than he had, but that wasn't it either. His dad was like a child in a lot of ways. Nicholas felt his father's fear, which soon dissipated. Nicholas knew for sure, for the first time, that he couldn't depend on his father to understand his deeper needs. He would get no help from that quarter. His father was afraid of the greater mysteries of life.

"I can't believe we caught a snake," Nicholas said too late in an attempt to bolster his dad.

His father looked sheepishly at him, his eyes glazed with embarrassment. He picked up his big blue plastic glass and sloshed it about as if the motion would make him look bolder, then held the mixed drink to his lips and took a long draught. That was it. It wasn't the snake that his father was afraid of, not really. He was just afraid of life, in a way that Nicholas could never be. There was something in his father's eyes that told the whole story. He had never really grown up.

At that moment Nicholas felt painfully aware of his lack of fear, as if he were the father, that his father was his son. They had traded places for a moment. His father was older, wiser in some ways, but about those hidden things that Nicholas found important, his father knew little. The mysteries of life scared his father and probably would for a long, long time to come. His father couldn't handle himself in the face of this kind of change. His interests lay elsewhere.

Nicholas' view of the world had cracked, a big crevice that widened inside him splitting him apart with dismay and emptiness. How would he make it without a grown-up to guide him? Everything hidden and new that he wanted to explore, he'd have to do without his family. What was worse, that would set him apart from them against his will. He had no choice. It appeared against impossible odds that his family feared him.

One thing was for certain then. He called upon his soul and gathered his courage. No, he wouldn't give in to doubt and despair. His latest discoveries had taught him that much. The scramble of his life could shake him about and tear him in two, but he believed then with all of his heart that he wouldn't give up. Even after his revealing shock that centered on the bull snake, he knew that he would be all right. He had a new sense of who he was.

CHAPTER EIGHT

Carol O'Malley picked the magazine up from atop the pile of mementos inside the old attic trunk. She kneeled there before the trunk in the attic, leafing through the pages and thinking about her experience with Nicholas, how he had known what she was going to read from the psychology of dreams article before she did, word for word. The episode had alarmed her so that she had locked the magazine up again. She wasn't sure just why she kept it here. It couldn't harm anyone. No, that wasn't the reason. She valued dreams more than she cared to admit or wished to explore. Dreams could be so painful. Better they should stay locked away like this magazine, than rushing about her mind, confusing and scaring her.

She looked down at the stack of mementos and gasped. The photograph of Ethan, her dearly departed son, struck her to heart. His radiant smile pierced her self-pity and rekindled her sorrow for him at the same time. His six-year-old face shone with joy and tenderness, his fine brown hair with its cowlick and his vulnerable eyes and sweet expression touched her. Ethan was part of the reason she didn't remember her dreams anymore. She had turned them off because she couldn't handle them. She wasn't even sure she could rekindle them if she wanted.

Her hopes for Ethan had died with him. She couldn't help it that life had crumbled around her, caving in on her at times. It seemed so unfair. She believed that there was life after death, but Ethan's memory choked her so. Could he still live on the other side?

A cloud of dust particles that she had stirred up and now floated in the sunlight streaming through the window, captured her imagination. She had forgotten how strong she felt about Ethan, pushing the memories of him away whenever they came up. Their time together had been brief, only six years; then he was gone. The pain of that passing lingered in her breast.

Around her lay dozens of cardboard boxes filled with keepsakes. Her husband William's army uniform wrapped in clear plastic hung on a nail from one of the rafters above. She didn't come up here very often, though the attic held so many of the mementos that were dear to her. The past held such a power over her that her eyes stung with tears. It all seemed to hit her at once along with the guilt that always preceded her worst thoughts. She had let Ethan die, let him drown. She deserved what she felt.

Everything felt jumbled inside her. The pain of her loss held her back too. The memories carried such weight that she felt she had drowned that fateful day at the Mississippi, not Ethan.

She had been sitting in a cane chair on the dock with Ethan, reading this very magazine on dreams, while he sat on a canvas chair, close to the edge of the dock fishing with a cane pole. She never suspected that anything so awful would happen. She never knew exactly how it happened, except that Ethan had caught a fish. He yelled out that he had, causing her to look up from her reading, only to see him falling, cane pole, canvas chair and all into the river, just a few feet below.

It didn't take long for her to react. She had thrown down the magazine and rushed for the edge of the dock. Looking down, she saw him thrashing about in the water, sinking fast. At six he still didn't know how to swim, nor did she at twenty-three. The sight of him several feet below the surface of the murky waters, which she knew to be at least twenty feet deep, shocked her to the core. She didn't know what to do. If she jumped in they both could drown. If she didn't, he most certainly would.

The current took him quickly, forcing him farther away, out closer to the main current of the dangerous Mississippi. He floated farther downstream as well where she knew he would encounter the bend in the river. She might grab him there as he floated near the sandy shore. She raced back up the dock to the riverbank and over to the shore, hoping with all of her might and praying to God that he would be close enough to save. When she got to the bend in the river, he had already floated by. She could just barely see his head above water now that she had come down off the dock and stood so much closer to water level. She kicked off her leather sandals and jumped in, knowing without a doubt that she had to act quickly without thinking about her fear of the water.

When she hit the cold river with a splash, she couldn't see Ethan, but she felt him nearby, knew that he must be there. She lost her footing as the current pulled her out too and she went under. Then she found him, grabbed hold of his shirt and tugged him close. But the current grew stronger, tugging at them both, but pulling them in separate directions even as she sought footing. Finally she found it, her bare feet striking the sandy bottom. She came up for a huge breath, gasping and choking. Ethan had gotten away. Petrified, she jumped back out into the river, not finding or seeing him, just groping like a mad woman, thrashing about as she had seen him do earlier, in hopes of catching him. With her eyes open underwater, she saw nothing but dark brown water through a dim light above.

She held her breath and flopped like a fish, wriggling this way and that, looking for the bottom. Finally she found the soft river bottom again, but this time without her son. She came up for air, standing on her toes as high as she could and sucking the refreshing air. Now she had a solid footing and she could push the water behind her with her hands and grope closer to the shore. With her head well above water, she turned and looked painfully out at the river. There was nothing but water, no Ethan, no sign of him at all. She had made it to solid ground, but he had not. That was too much to bear. The shock had her and like a zombie, she walked slowly toward the shore, knowing only one thing, that her son was lost. Just a few feet away from dry land, she turned and shouted, "Ethan, Ethan, come back." She knew it was no use. Ethan was gone, maybe not even dead yet, just struggling as she had, but worse.

She collapsed on the dry riverbank gasping for air, half in and half out of the water that lapped against her, pushing her. She felt nothing but despair, her heart broken. She got up then, dripping wet and stood tall, craning her neck, looking for him as far out as she could, but he was gone. She would never see him again. She had failed him. She had lived and he had not. She would never see him again.

That was how it happened. She had replayed that memory every day for a long time, until she could stand it no longer and the edge wore off. Now all she had was broken dreams and bitterness to cling to, at least that was the way it seemed. Perhaps Nicholas could help. She had pushed him away with her awful reaction to his strange ability to know her words before she did. No one had ever done that to her before. She knew he was a good boy though. He always had been. But she was mixed up. Her insides churned with guilt and anxiety. She had to get help somewhere.

CHAPTERN NINE

Lucy hop scotched across the black and white checkered tiles on their kitchen floor. "A nick in time saves time," she repeated over and over as she jumped from one square to another. Nicholas leaned against the sink with arms crossed, watching her. He knew the true phrase was "a stitch in time saves nine" or "just in the nick of time," but not the parts of the two separate phrases pieced together. She had such a wonderful way of combining things. Some people called him Nick, but only those closest to him.

"What do you suppose that means?" he asked. She glanced at him without stopping, hopping from one square to the next, totally entranced by her invention.

"A nick in time saves nine," she said as if to aggravate him. She jumped lightly like a pixie, her hair bouncing across her face, obscuring her vision, which she obviously didn't rely on. She never stepped on a line the whole time as she jumped from one square to another, then reaching the wall by the window, turned, hunched her shoulders up once in a shrug for dramatic effect and came back toward him.

"I've never seen a ghost," Nicholas said hoping to jar her. Earlier in the day, Lucy had told him that once she had seen her great-great-grandfather Ruben's spirit in their house, but

73

Nicholas hadn't believed her. Actually, he just said that he didn't believe her to tease her. Everything about ghosts fascinated him really. He had never seen one and felt embarrassed by the fact.

A growing tension that gathered inside him threatened to burst. God, Lucy could get to him! He wanted to do something that would get her attention. Sensing his dilemma, Lucy stopped and looked at him hard, her hair falling in its rightful place over one eye, making her other eye look all the more intense. That was Lucy, intense. Feeling unhinged with mischief, he ran into the bathroom and grabbed a large red towel from the rack on the wall, then ran back out into the kitchen. He held the towel out in front of him with both hands, feeling clever and stuck out his chest like a matador.

Lucy took up the challenge. She put down her head and snorted like a bull, pawing at the floor with her foot. Nicholas loved the way she responded to his lead, especially the snorting that he found so realistic. Her nostrils flared and her face actually turned red. How did she do it? She could change in a second, just like he did.

She charged at him across the floor, but just as she was about to run into him, he stepped to the side, swishing the towel away before her as he spun about. She turned and charged again. He repeated his performance, spinning about, but this time as she passed, he stuck out his foot and tripped her. She missed a step and plunged to the floor where she landed on her side, her skirt hiked up high and her face flushed with exasperation. He hadn't meant to be so devilish, but the invitation was too inviting.

Her reddened face turned white as she gave him a cold stare that worried him. Then she smiled wide and he knew it was all right. She didn't mind.

"Sorry," Nicholas said, still feeling slightly uncomfortable. Lucy laid back full length on the floor, looking at the ceiling and clasping her hands over her chest. Then she closed her eyes and let her head fall to the side motionless as if she had died.

Nicholas loved the way she egged him on. Sometimes he thought she was so cute, even beautiful and quite feminine, and then she'd pull a funny stunt like this. In these moments, she didn't appear to be a girl or a guy, just a crazy person that intrigued him.

"My turn," he said, draping the towel across her face, teasing her with it. "You be the matador and give me a turn at the bull. She didn't move. He reached down and tickled her beneath her arm, accidentally feeling the uncomfortable presence of her bra strap beneath her blue silk blouse. Still, she didn't move. She was dead.

"Hmm, what can I do to a dead person that would break the spell?" he asked, feeling impish. He poked her in the stomach softly as if inspecting a lump of bread dough then poked her again, watching her face all the while for any signs of life. No reaction, but then her lips twitched with the hint of a smile at the corner of her mouth. She liked it, this playing dead. He put his hand on her stomach and rocked her back and forth, watching her mouth curl up in a pleasing smile. This could become interesting. He reached back and tickled her bare foot. She sprang up then at the waist, still stiff like a corpse with her arms outstretched and her eyes still closed, just inches away from Nicholas.

"Come on, little Miss Muffin," he said. "It's your turn to be the matador." He felt a mixture of fear and excitement at being so close to her. Lucy relaxed then, opened her eyes and looked softly into his. Her expression so rich with opportunity unnerved Nicholas completely. He got up off the floor and looked down upon her, feeling helpless and wondering what to do next. He might be passing up something wonderful, but he wasn't sure of himself. He'd never been so close to a girl before, not like this.

He had to put distance between him and her. The thick towel was a welcome diversion in his hands as he twirled it up into a tight whip, pulled it back and playfully threatened her with it. She got up slowly and brushed herself off, an act so graceful and purely feminine that he blushed. She didn't give up. He didn't feel nearly as tough as he wanted to.

"Okay, hot shot," she said, switching characters once again as she grabbed at the towel. He let her pull it away and stepped backwards to the wall, feeling stupid, as if he had missed the chance of a lifetime. Lucy unrolled the towel and held it out before her like a matador's cape. She looked stubbornly at him with her feet firmly planted, all femininity gone.

Feeling completely off balance, Nicholas took up her challenge and raced at the towel, which she easily flicked behind her as she twirled to her left. He charged headlong past her, his momentum carrying him on toward the threshold of the pantry, where with a dull thud and a jolt of pain, he slammed his bare toe into the doorjamb. Hundreds of tiny stars exploded all about his head as he fell to the floor on his back. God, that hurt!

Looking up through tears, he saw the oddest thing. A man floated in the faint light of the pantry between several shelves of pickled condiments and a stack of old picnic coolers. Nicholas could just make him out. He wasn't a real man, not a physical man anyway. He floated in the air somehow, a fluid yet distinct shape that surprised him.

Nicholas realized that the man was a spirit. It was unlikely that it was Lucy's great-great-grandfather though. This man had black skin. He had to be someone else. The spirit's face shone sleek with sweat as if he had been working very hard, the loose folds of his hanging jowls adding to an impression of weariness. His big watery eyes looked upon Nicholas with great sympathy. The apparition's wide shoulders looked solid and his powerful arms hung long past his tattered sleeves. His hands though caught Nicholas' attention for sure. Strong and large, capable hands, they looked as if they could grasp anything. The man looked as if he could reach out with care and take away ones heaviest load.

Lucy came to Nicholas' aid then, bending over him and pressing her hands tightly around his bloody foot. He strained his mind, wishing to see the man more clearly. The whites of the man's eyes stood out more than anything as he stared wide with recognition at Nicholas lying on the pantry floor. "Nicholas," Lucy cried putting his foot in her lap. "Nicholas!" Nicholas paid her little attention. He wanted to know who the man was. He didn't want to lose the vision, but he did. The man had faded and was gone.

CHAPTER TEN

Nicholas didn't forget about the spirit he'd seen, but his injury had to be taken care of. His mother drove him downtown to the doctor's office, where the doctor deadened his toe with Novocain. Then the doctor proceeded to pull off the toenail while Nicholas watched on somewhat horrified. The gory operation caused him even more agony than the injury.

Afterwards he lay about for a day or so, just long enough to please his mother and think about his pigheadedness. Maybe he deserved the injury for teasing Lucy the way he had, though she had shown no real sign of being bothered by his headstrong ways. Sometimes he pushed too hard, like just before the big toe accident. His attraction to Lucy had caused trouble. If it hadn't been for that attraction, he wouldn't have been so compelled to tease her. He either had to do that or deal with her face to face, so to speak.

Summer came as school let out, giving Nicholas a lot of free time to do as he wished. Lucy's and his dream pact had been so successful that they agreed to try another experiment. Lucy still talked about her great-great grandfather Ruben as well as the more recent ghost that had showed up in their pantry. She'd never seen that spirit before. Nicholas wanted to see both spirits if possible. Fear wouldn't stop him, since he had very little fear of ghosts. He figured it was okay if after a person died they came to you as a spirit, unless maybe they were an evil person. That would not be okay. In any case some part of him knew that he would be all right. He had a sixth sense for steering away from evil and believed in the protection of Christ. His experiences and years of study in church had given him that.

Nicholas also knew that people weren't always what they appeared to be on the surface either. He also feared that he might not be able to see a ghost so easily. Just how did you make that happen anyway? He hardly thought that a painful injury was a very good way. He definitely believed that some people could see ghosts when they chose to. Of course he could have imagined the ghost in the pantry just because he wanted to see one so bad, but that didn't seem possible. The true test would be if Lucy and he both saw her great-great-grandfather Ruben's ghost. Maybe then they could compare notes.

He had blown his chance to find out what Lucy had seen in the pantry when he stubbed his toe. In his excitement, he had told Lucy everything that he had seen first, describing the ghost in detail without thinking. Lucy said she saw the spirit too, but she could have just been trying to make him feel good. He didn't think so though. The way she looked at him when she told him things made him believe her. Nobody was more serious than Lucy when she wanted to be, of course unless it was Nicholas' mother or father when they were chewing him out for something bad he might have done.

Lucy had told him the story of her Grandfather Ruben and how just before the Civil War, he had acted as a spiritual medium for some folks, which upset a lot of others. Spiritual mediums were people that could talk to the dead, those on the "other side" as it was called. Nicholas found the term "the other side" amusing. It suggested to him that he lived on this side a distinction he found difficult to imagine. What did he know of the other side anyway? In the old days, as in the present, some people didn't think talking to spirits was a good thing. They figured if you did, you were inviting the devil into your life; that is of course unless you talked to those spirits they called the Saints. Nicholas figured that Jesus could qualify as a spirit, even a ghost. Most people's definition of a ghost usually involved something scary or evil though.

Lucy also told him that her great-great-grandfather Ruben had been a slave runner for the Underground Railroad, helping slaves from the South find their way to freedom in the North. Very few people knew that Ruben had been a slave runner, but it did come out some years later, long after the war when people didn't care quite so much.

Determined to call up a ghost, Nicholas and Lucy decided to meet in the pantry that following Thursday. Lucy's parents always square danced at the Moose Lodge on that night, so Nicholas and Lucy would have her parent's house to themselves.

Nicholas felt that something good would happen. He wanted to see a ghost when he wasn't in pain or in some other strange state like a dream. He wished to see the spirit of someone that he knew had once been a physical person, like Lucy's Great Grandfather Ruben. Lucy and Nicholas could prove that Ruben not only existed, but also had a definite history and character. Nicholas didn't know exactly why he wanted to see a ghost, but he had a few ideas.

An interest in the invisible worlds had arisen in him, growing stronger daily, ever since he'd seen Tyco in his dream. Now this ghost had appeared and fueled the fire that already raged inside him. He felt that the spirits could help him understand life and his new sense of purpose, those things that his father and mother could only give him a basic understanding of. With Tyco and the new spirits' help, he might learn about the many mysteries that always intrigued him. For instance, where did people go after they died and what was it that made people so afraid of death? Most people that he knew weren't that interested or open to such things.

Thursday night's meeting with Lucy meant everything to Nicholas. The more he got to know Lucy, the more he liked her. It was unusual for Nicholas to be so taken with anyone, unless you could include his sweet old grandmother who had passed away some years back. His heart had always skipped with happiness when he saw her. But she was a lot different than Lucy. In her practical way, his Grandmother had done things for him to show Nicholas her love. No one other than Nicholas had the ability to see things the way Lucy did though, at least that he knew anyway.

When Thursday finally came, Nicholas hobbled over to Lucy's on his crutches and knocked quietly on the inside back porch door. Lucy let him into the kitchen without a word. Nicholas felt electricity between them, ripe with promise.

"I'll have to leave the pantry door open just a little bit," Lucy explained as they entered the dark pantry. "My little sister's asleep upstairs and I have to listen in case she wakes up. Lucy gave Nicholas a hard look. Her long black hair stretched back behind her head in a ponytail made her face appear more intense than ever.

The pantry door gave the two of them quite a tussle and Nicholas' crutches got in the way, but they managed to break it loose an inch or two from its original position, scraping against the gritty linoleum and sending chills up his spine.

"Let's stop for a second," Nicholas said, gripping his crutches by their handles and backing up away from the door. He figured it had probably been years since anyone had even tried to budge the door. "It'll take a while to get that thing to move very far. His big toe throbbed and he felt like lying down, but a deal was a deal. Lucy and he had agreed to this meeting. "Are you sure we need to close it any farther?" he asked. "I want it to be darker in here so we can see the spirits easier," Lucy replied. She pulled at the door and the smooth muscles in her slender arms strained, but the door wouldn't move.

Nicholas joined her, knowing the effort would only make his toe throb more painfully. "It's going to be hard to open very quickly if your sister wakes up," he said between clenched teeth as he pulled hard on the door. The door broke free then and moved easily across the uneven flooring. Now it wouldn't matter if Lucy's sister woke up. They could open the door as fast as they wanted. Lucy and Nicholas sat in the dark pantry with just a beam of light from the kitchen streaming through a crack between the doorframe and the door. Lucy sat upon an old wooden pickle barrel and Nicholas upon two large plastic picnic coolers. Between them they had set up a rough and dusty board table. The enclosed space of the pantry felt safe and secure, hidden from prying eyes.

I hope that ghost comes back," Nicholas said as he watched Lucy take down a small white candle from one of the shelves beside them. She moved so gracefully, placing the candle exactly in the center of the board as if she measured the distances with a special power. She took out a wooden match from its container and struck it suddenly upon the side. The brilliance of the exploding match flame and the following puff of burnt sulfur engulfed Nicholas' senses.

Lucy touched the flaming match to the candlewick, her face now glorious in the bright light. She might be a girl and a beautiful one at that, but she did things as he did, always extra aware of her surroundings. The candle gave off a tiny flame at first, then flickered and slowly grew, illuminating the pantry around them. Nicholas calmed himself and thought of their purpose for coming here. "I thought I could chant Ruben's name out loud while we concentrate on him," he said, feeling awkward. Lucy didn't respond which made him feel even more awkward. Then Nicholas remembered that he had called upon Tyco out by the stream and that had worked. Would that qualify him as a medium? He hardly thought so. Well, maybe Tyco wasn't a ghost, because he had never died that Nicholas knew of. Ghosts were supposed to be the spirits of the dead. Nevertheless, remembering his success with Tyco assured Nicholas. "Ruben, Ruben," he repeated out loud, "please come now. The words came out sounding flat to Nicholas. He felt foolish. What was he supposed to do?

Lucy reached around the candle on both sides and took hold of his hands. The candle flame rose as if an invisible force pulled it up toward the ceiling. Nicholas instantly felt an energy emanating from Lucy's hands come into his own. The energy traveled up into his arms, then all through his body, helping him to let go of his doubts and concentrate.

Everything in the room centered on the candle flame. The more Nicholas concentrated upon it, the higher it became. He felt the energy between himself and Lucy grow stronger, so strong as they sat there, that it felt as if he could fly. His hands and arms vibrated as the connection between their hands intensified. The candle flame grew fantastically high. At one point, for a moment, he lost his concentration, thinking that the spirit of Ruben might not appear. He feared that would make the experiment fail, but he could feel that Lucy took up the slack, sending him even more energy than before. The rays of golden candlelight shot out like a small sun, a central beacon that radiated pure energy. Lucy and his mind were one now. He could feel it. No doubts could separate them.

A shocking blue sphere of light about an inch wide appeared above Lucy's head! The amazing sphere, so unearthly in its exquisite beauty and hue, moved over between Lucy and him off to his left. This was a first. He had never seen such a thing!

Nicholas squeezed Lucy's hands in excitement, but the blue sphere of light disappeared. Lucy's soothing presence quickly calmed him. Where the sphere had been to his left, he could now make out the image of someone. It appeared to be a man. His head and shoulders formed more clearly and Nicholas could tell that it was the old black fellow he had seen before.

Nicholas glanced at Lucy. She saw the spirit too. She was looking right at him!

Lucy closed her eyes and Nicholas followed her lead. The little blue sphere of light appeared in his mind's eye, and then was gone. The old black man appeared where the sphere had been. Nicholas marveled at the way he could concentrate to see more clearly the dark skinned face and bright eyes of the kindly old fellow. Even the outline of the man's body showed clearly now. Several times the vision dimmed until Nicholas would concentrate harder to make the spirit come back into focus. Nicholas' breath deepened and slowed as he relaxed completely and allowed himself to actually feel the essence of the spirit. The old man who might at one time have been a slave was definitely not a defeated or weak person. The spirit communed with Nicholas at first, offering him strength and wisdom without saying a word. As Nicholas made the silent mind to mind contact, the spirit said, "You ah da Terra Champeen.

Nicholas accepted the message, which gave him a sense of fulfillment, even though he didn't know exactly what it meant. If he remembered right, Terra was the Italian word for Earth. Since some people in the old South had that funny way of talking, champeen must mean champion. The spirit had called him the Earth Champion. Nicholas opened his eyes again, curious beyond belief, to see what Lucy was doing. The candle's glow made her face look peaceful and sweet. Her concentration, though relaxed, seemed total.

Nicholas left his eyes open and brought the spirit of the old man into focus again. Though seeing the spirit was harder with his eyes open, he could still feel with his mind and bring the image clearly into shape. Several shades of deep gold and green light moved slowly about the head and shoulders of the figure like electric water.

Nicholas could actually see through the spirit's form to the pantry shelves behind it, but when he focused again, he realized that a new spirit had appeared where the other one had been.

The new spirit wore a bow tie, a black symbol that stood out at first like a figure eight lying on its side. It reminded Nicholas of the sign for infinity. He could also see that the spirit wore a sleek black tuxedo and a brilliant red cummerbund around his waist. Nicholas could barely make out the spirit's face, but he could see that it was a man and that he sported a well-trimmed handle bar moustache. Nicholas let go completely and the image became much clearer. It seemed the less he tried, the better his concentration worked and the better he could see.

The spirit's jet-black hair parted just off-center in an old world style that was well combed and glossy with oil. His small and dark deep-set eyes startled Nicholas with a powerful energy as they looked deeply into his own. This man had to know something!

Nicholas closed his eyes then and the spirit spoke to his mind. "I am Ruben. My teacher who just spoke to you is called Abraxas."

The clarity of the message tickled Nicholas, but he didn't open his eyes or squirm one bit. Though Abraxas looked tattered and old, his simple and loving manner had impressed Nicholas greatly.

Without thinking, Nicholas let go of Lucy's hands. He had the distinct feeling that she received a message of her own. It would be good to know just what that was, but later. He had to take full advantage of this opportunity. Somehow he knew that holding hands wasn't necessary anymore.

He leaned back against the cool stucco wall behind him. The spirit had disappeared. Nicholas knew he could find him again. He crossed his legs Indian style on top of the picnic cooler, being careful not to jar his foot covered with two thick socks to protect his sore big toe. He closed his eyes and breathed deep. Even before he saw Ruben, the messages began. "There are two things that you need to see," the spirit said, and then paused. Nicholas placed his hands on his knees and straightened his spine like a yogi in meditation, feeling grateful and enthused to talk with Ruben.

Lucy stirred about in her place across the board. Nicholas' neck felt tense with the prospect of losing contact with Ruben. He willed it to relax. Two images came to him then, a small copper coin lying in the dirt and a small carved wooden box.

"Beneath the back porch," Ruben explained. That was all Nicholas heard. Ruben must have gone. When he opened his eyes, and saw Lucy smiling at him, his heart leaped. Though he didn't understand all of the messages, Lucy and he had succeeded. They had talked to the spirits!

CHAPTER ELEVEN

ee what I mean?" Lucy said, pointing at the first page of the Bible. She held it open in her lap, a thick and heavy leather bound edition, dusty and faded with age. Nicholas sat beside her on the couch in Lucy's living room, but he could barely make out the writing near her fingertip. The cloudy day afforded little light and the long narrow windows partially covered with burgundy velvet curtains made the room darker.

Lucy turned on the antique stained glass lamp sitting on an end table beside her. Nicholas crossed one leg over the other, feeling the ever-present throb of his sore toe and leaned closer to her over the book to get a better look. On the page, many hand written names filled the branches of the family tree. Lucy pointed at a name penned in a beautiful cursive style: Ruben Montgomery, born 1830, died 1911. Lucy slowly lifted the Bible and placed it, still open, in Nicholas' lap. Then she got up, causing Nicholas to rock about on the rickety old couch. Regaining his balance, he watched her walk from the old Persian rug across the hardwood floor, her footsteps ringing out against the plaster walls and high ceiling. She stopped before the fireplace. Then slowly as if in a dream, she raised her arm to the fireplace mantle and gently settled her fingers on the gilded frame of a small photograph.

Lucy could be a younger version of her mother Grace. Lucy's long full dress, an old flowered print that her mother might have once worn, fit her well. Lucy borrowed Grace's memories and experiences and made them her own. These family records meant everything to her. Lucy's face, bright with joy, warmed Nicholas as she returned with the prized photo in her hand to the couch. She sat down beside him, scooted over so close to him that he lost his breath. This must be what adults felt with each other sometimes. Sharing her history gave Lucy a glow he found contagious. He imagined himself married to her, an adult 20 something that had just been accepted into Lucy's family. His pleasant fantasy was crushed when Lucy handed him the picture. Something inside said that Lucy and he would not always be around each other.

"This is great-great grandfather Ruben," she said.

"Cool," Nicholas said, feeling suddenly awkward. Lucy's grandfather certainly looked handsome and capable dressed in a suit with his hair parted down the middle and moustache gleaming. "Your grandfather doesn't look very old," he added, feeling dumb. The photograph had probably been taken a hundred years ago. "He looks a lot like he did when I saw him in the pantry last night," Nicholas said. "Is that how you saw him?"

Lucy didn't take her eyes off the picture, but she nodded and gave him a half smile, a wistful look, as if she barely heard him. "It's so hard to describe how the spirits really look," she said. "Sometimes I have an image of one in my mind, but it's so different from a photograph or how you and I appear to each other.

"I know what you mean," Nicholas said, feeling more at ease. "It's like the spirits are made out of light. I even saw a bright blue light before I saw the first spirit.

Lucy looked interested.

"There was this blue sphere about an inch or so wide," he said, "hovering in the air on my left just before I saw him. And when I saw the spirit appear, he looked so wispy, like he was all color and made out of light too. I've never seen anything like that sphere before. It's different than any light or color in this world. Nicholas fingered the long sleeve of his shirt. "I mean the color of green in this shirt is pretty and bright, but nothing near as beautiful as the colors I saw last night.

"What did Abraxas say to you?" Lucy asked. Nicholas pursed his lips and let out a big sigh. "He called me the Terra Champeen. All of a sudden it occurred to him that Lucy had called the spirit Abraxas. He hadn't told her anything about last night's experiences until now. Just after their session with the spirits, Lucy's parents had come home, so Lucy and he didn't have a chance to talk about what had happened. Lucy had heard the spirit's name just like he had! Wow! His whole world felt right side up for a change. "Did he tell you his name?" he asked. Lucy moved as if in slow motion as she raised her head and looked at him. She smiled wide, her eyes lit with friendship and nodded. Nicholas pushed himself up from the couch and stood on one leg, balancing precariously as he thrashed his arms wildly about. "My God Lucy. Do you know what this means?"

Lucy smiled even wider.

"The spirits are real!" Nicholas shouted. "Of course they're real," she said. "I've always known that.

Nicholas grabbed his crutches that leaned on his end of the couch, fit them beneath his armpits and launched himself across the rug. When he reached the end of the rug, he spun quickly about and launched himself forward again. He did this time and again with great coordination even though the rug slid freely beneath him. The spirits were real!

"You don't understand Lucy," he said feeling refreshed. His foot even felt better. He pressed it to the floor in an attempt to walk on it, wishing it was healed more now than ever. He had to do something with all of his newfound energy. There was so much that he wanted to do. He leaned his crutches against the fireplace and with head down, continued to pace, limping to be sure, but gaining strength and smoothing his gait as he did so. Lucy and his experiment with the spirits had given him renewed hope. "I've spent my whole life wondering about that," he said scratching his head. When he looked up, Lucy was smiling again. She didn't think him silly at all. Her way of seeing things could be so darned wonderful. It made him want to jump out of his skin. Every step that he took became steadier. He stretched his toes and arched his injured foot, then placed it back on the rug. He had been afraid to use it. His toe felt weak, but okay. He could walk freely now though somewhat uneven. The thick sole of his Earth shoe raised his right leg so that his left leg appeared shorter. He walked like Long John Silver with a wooden peg leg.

"There's something I have to show you," he said, grabbing the crutches. "Let's go to my house and get me another shoe and my bicycle. There's some place I have to show you."

At Nicholas' house, Lucy stood over him, watching as he sat on his bed and squeezed his foot into the mate to his other shoe. Nicholas' toe didn't hurt so much, though he knew better than to get too cocky. That had caused him to bang his toe in the first place.

Once outside on his bicycle, Nicholas felt fully charged like a knight ready for battle. Lucy had changed her dress and now wore a tight pair of Levi blue jeans, the same deep color as his. She rode beside him on her bike, the pink streamers on her handle grips flying in the breeze. The sun came out and the clouds began to disappear. They took highway ninety north of town, the blacktop a long straight string of licorice that would take them to Nicholas' favorite place.

They climbed a long low hill for about a mile with a broad prairie pasture on one side and a plowed field on the other. Ahead of them on the horizon, a long line of cottonwood trees gave cover for deer, pheasants and many other animals that lived at the river. How could one not love this country? The open air and warmth, the smell of the green Earth, it all spelled freedom and pleasure, an exciting adventure that one could enjoy without even trying.

Lucy looked excited. She rode the bike as well as any boy, her long legs rapidly pumping upon the pedals. Nicholas rose up high on one pedal and the gear slipped. He fell, but caught himself just before he hit the crossbar. Strangely enough, he'd had the bike fixed only a week ago. He adjusted the gear level on the lower rung of his handlebars. The gears shouldn't be slipping in and out by themselves like that. He couldn't shake the feeling that something was wrong, that he had just missed being hurt again. This time he didn't think he had done anything to deserve it. There was a difference between being careless and things failing themselves. No, the closer Lucy and he got to the stream, the more he thought something was screwy.

Up ahead by the stream, a cloud of dust over the trees looked suspicious. It could be smoke, but he didn't think so. The cloud didn't look dark enough, more like those he'd seen over the plows or crust busters dragged behind tractors in the open field. Nevertheless, he couldn't wait to show Lucy the old hollow tree. The sound of a tractor's engine floated on the breeze as they approached the creek. Lucy and he took the dirt road just past the highway bridge, then the four-wheel drive trail that meandered down to it. After a while, they found a game trail where they could walk on their bikes through the tall weeds by the creek. Finally they were out of earshot of the highway and the dirt road where they couldn't hear any traffic. They laid their bikes down on their sides in the tall grass at the top of a hill above the creek.

Nicholas looked down below to his favorite spot and his world collapsed. Everything had been destroyed! He started down the hill, walking slowly, taking it all in, numbed at the sight.

Across the creek, a huge yellow bulldozer came alive with a shocking pop of its engine and started scraping away at the virgin sand hills. The magic old hollow tree lay chopped in pieces on the ground. Tyco would never sit high on its branch again. The bulldozers and land scrapers had done their jobs well. Nicholas' favorite place had become a barren field! The birds had fled. Not one could be seen or heard. The chugging of the horrible tractor engine made him shudder.

Almost all the water in the stream was gone. A few fish flopped miserably about. Several carp still struggling for their last breaths, thrashed about in a puddle of water much too shallow to sustain them. Many other fish lay still on their muddy deathbeds.

Evidently, whoever had destroyed the land had dammed up the water somewhere upstream, probably for irrigation or some other grand purpose. Whoever had done the damage must be planning to farm the area, put in wheat or milo, but why so close to the stream? That didn't make sense, unless they intended to never let the stream run again. If they did, it might flood their fields in the spring.

Nicholas couldn't blame the farmers really. This was the doing of a large corporation, which was just a part of something larger, a system that rolled over the Earth without thinking or remorse. The farmers only followed the rules of the system. Most of them were good and simple people. Many of them were going out of business, making way for a cold future that made Nicholas' skin crawl.

Lucy walked beside him to the spot where the hollow tree had once stood. Somehow the hole in the ground beneath the trunk had disappeared. Even the stump and the roots had been cut up into chunks. What an awful day! Nicholas slumped to the ground before the pieces of tree; his head bent downward, a swell of anxiety rising in his chest. He felt sorry for the Earth and guilty for being a human. Humans had done this awful thing. They destroyed the Earth wherever they went. He picked up a section of tree root and held it to his chest. Lucy knelt beside him, and placed her hand gently on his shoulder. A surge of anger made her hand feel hot upon him. This wasn't supposed to happen. He didn't want to get used to a life where the land was destroyed. He wanted it to live. He clenched his jaw and ground it from side to side. "What did I do wrong?" he asked, shaking his head in disbelief.

Nicholas tried to imagine how the place had looked a few days ago when he'd been there last, how splendid the country had been. He felt foolish. The destruction of the place had robbed his good humor so easily. What would Lucy think? What had he done to cause this?

With a sweeping gesture of his hand at the countryside, he said, "This is my favorite spot I was telling you about.

She searched his eyes sympathetically. "You didn't do anything, Nicholas. It's not your fault."

Nicholas looked over to the creek bed where a big carp lying on its side pathetically flicked its tail, its exposed orange and white belly drying in the heat. The fish was tormented. The fish and he both had a connection to the Earth. They were both dependent on it. The Earth gave him and everyone upon it all that they needed. No longer would he consider himself separated from the Earth. The Earth was as alive as any person, a living being that moved and had a purpose.

"We could save some of these fish," he said with a glimmer of hope as he rubbed the root with his thumb. He got up from his knees and walked over to the creek bank. Lucy followed and stood beside him. They watched the carp gasping and sucking for air, its pale gills moving up and down like a bellows. "My uncle has a pond out on his ranch that we might be able to put them in," he said.

"Let's do it, Nicholas," Lucy said. "If we hurry, we might be able to save quite a few.

It took longer than Nicholas wanted to rush back to town and call his Uncle Caleb, but his spirits lifted when his uncle told him he'd be right over to fetch them in his pick-up. Nicholas felt strange once the three of them got back to the creek and started picking up the dying fish. They did the best they could, piling the fish into a bunch of gunnysacks. Maybe some of the fish would survive, but some wouldn't.

Caleb stooped over, picking up fish after fish without complaint. He helped Lucy and Nicholas for quite a while, though they worked as quickly as they could.

In his perspiration-stained cowboy hat and boots, Uncle Caleb looked like the guy in the Marlboro cigarette commercials. But Nicholas' uncle was the real thing. Uncle Caleb owned his own ranch east of town and knew firsthand about the countryside. The corners of his eyes were locked in a permanent squint that stretched his whole face, a hardened result of many years outdoors. Occasionally his uncle would spit a long streak of tobacco juice into a creek puddle with a splash, then lick his lips and continue his chew, picking up fish as if he did it every day.

Nicholas couldn't handle chewing tobacco himself (it tasted like a cross between hot mustard and pipe tobacco) but he praised his uncle silently for helping out. Nicholas knew that his uncle wouldn't want to be complimented at a time like this. That wasn't his way.

"I hope you know that we are saving your life," his uncle said with a grin to a channel catfish that he held up in his hand. He placed the fish in his empty gunnysack and closed the top, then wiped his hands on his Wrangler jeans and hoisted the sack back over his shoulder. Nicholas walked beside his tall slender uncle, feeling small, but glad. Though Nicholas' favorite place had been destroyed, this last ditch effort to save the fish made him feel better. He might not like sitting out where the hollow tree had been anymore, but at least he could go to his uncle's ranch and visit the fish that survived. Lucy looked at him from across the creek bed, her hair partially covering her face. She looked tired and mud streaked, her clothes and skin smeared with grime. She carried a gunny sack bulging with fish over her shoulder as she walked forward self-contained, a trouper to be sure. Maybe the world wasn't such a bad place. Nicholas had people like Uncle Caleb and Lucy.

If there was one thing Nicholas had learned, it was that he didn't know much. He didn't know why humans, like the ones that destroyed the land, could be so careless. How did you not be a part of that carelessness? Nicholas couldn't stop being human, but he didn't have to be blind to the needs of the Earth and her many creatures.

CHAPTER TWELVE

"Pull off some slats," Lucy said, looking about to see if the neighbors watched. Nicholas squatted in the grass before the latticework, his hammer ready. Lucy's great-great-grandfather Ruben had told them beneath the back porch, but the only way under it was through the latticework. "We'll replace them when we're done," she added. "Nobody will ever know the difference.

Nicholas quickly pried off first one of the slats, then several more to make a hole big enough to crawl through. "I thought your parents would never leave," he said, getting down on his knees before the hole. Lucy's parents had finally gone to one of their Sunday afternoon Bible study groups. Now Lucy and he could have fun. Ever since Lucy's Great Grandfather Ruben had talked to them a few days earlier, Nicholas had wanted to look under the porch to see what they would find. Ruben might have been talking about a different porch, but Nicholas hoped not. It made more sense that it would be Lucy's, since Ruben had lived in her house once, long ago. A thousand and one cobweb strands prevented his easy entry, sticking to every part of him. He didn't like the feel of them on his face, but he pushed through with his hands and crawled forward beneath the porch. A little sunlight filtered in through the diamond shaped patterns of the latticework, but not enough to see much. He flicked on his flashlight and shone it about. Dust filled his nostrils. A couple of moths fluttered away as he crawled around to get a better look. He didn't know exactly where or how to begin. Ruben's information, though clear, had not been very detailed.

"Do you see anything?" Lucy asked softly. She squatted down and looked at him through the hole in the latticework that he'd made. They weren't breaking any laws or anything, but one had to be careful where adults were concerned. They got upset so easily. Adults might not appreciate the fact that Lucy and he talked to spirits.

"Not yet," he replied, sitting on his butt with his head bent down to keep from hitting the two by fours propping up the porch floor. This could be a real wild goose chase. Nicholas remembered his vision of the carved wooden box buried in the dirt. The box must be down here somewhere. Better to start at the center and work outward, go over every inch with the light to look for some sort of clue.

He crawled a few feet to the center of the porch. That's where he would have buried something, right in the center. Do you guys have anything to dig with?" he asked her, "something small enough to work with down here?"

Graceful and as silent as a lynx, Lucy got up from her haunches and rushed off toward the back of the garage. She returned moments later with a small army surplus shovel. He loosened the screw action on the handle and opened the shovel blade up halfway, then tightened the screw.

Nicholas used the shovel like a pick and easily dug into the soft earth beneath the porch. He took his time and screened every bit of loose dirt with his fingertips, hoping to find the coin he'd seen in his vision. Ruben hadn't said the coin was buried in the dirt, but it wouldn't hurt to look.

It didn't take long to find something, a small hard object, round like a coin, but too covered with dirt to be sure. He rubbed away at the dry earth with his thumb, uncovering a copper colored metal and the tarnished profile of an Indian chief, complete with feathered headdress. Nicholas could only make out the numbers one and eight below the Indian's head. This had to be the coin he had seen in his vision, an Indian head penny from the eighteen hundreds!

Nicholas crawled over to Lucy and handed the coin to her. Her eyes grew wide as she inspected it closely in the sunlight. "Wow, this is something!" she said. "You told me you saw a coin like this. Maybe the box is buried underneath.

Nicholas crawled back beneath the porch to the center once again and continued digging. This time he wouldn't be so concerned with every little dirt clod. The back end of the flashlight fit well in his mouth and freed up his hands to shovel.

It was easy work, picking away at the dirt and piling it off to the side of the hole he'd made. Before too long the blade of his shovel hit something hard with a thud. He leaned over the hole and shined his flashlight down into it. There might be a tree root or some piece of trash left when Lucy's ancestors built the house.

He unscrewed the shovel and straightened out the blade so he could dig deeper. His shovel blade hit something large and hard at the bottom of the hole. He couldn't tell what at first, but he soon gasped in astonishment when he realized he had uncovered a small wooden box.

He used his fingers to free the small rectangular shaped box and pulled it up, proud of himself. The box looked rotten in places, but still whole, about four inches wide and maybe ten inches long. He crawled over to Lucy, holding it high in one hand.

"You found it," she said, jumping up and down. "You found the box. What do you thinks inside it?" she asked as he handed it to her.

"I don't know," Nicholas said, "but I can't wait to find out." He turned about and got down on his hands and knees again. "I better cover up that hole though so nobody finds it.

After filling in the hole and tamping the dirt down with the flat of the shovel, Nicholas crawled back out from beneath the porch and started to repair the latticework. I didn't see the coin or the box like you did in your vision," Lucy commented.

Nicholas tapped a nail back into its original place in one of the wooden slats. He shrugged his shoulders. "That doesn't matter though, I guess," he said. "Does it?"

Lucy stood beside him fingering the lid of the box. "Not really," she replied.

"What did Abraxas and Ruben say to you?" Nicholas asked. "You never did tell me everything they said.

"The main thing was about you," Lucy said.

Nicholas suddenly felt uncomfortable, as if he had done something wrong. He remembered what the spirits had told him, but he didn't know just what Lucy would come up with.

"They called you the Terra Champion," Lucy said.

Some of Nicholas' discomfort faded, though he wasn't sure he liked the idea of being the Terra Champion. What was the Earth Champion anyway? It all sounded so heavy and serious.

After he finished repairing the latticework, Lucy led him through the back porch door and into the house. They walked quietly through the cool kitchen and tip toed up the carpeted stair way even though they both knew nobody else was around.

Lucy's bedroom full of sunshine and a pleasant breeze coming in the window relaxed Nicholas. Lucy brought out some newspapers from her closet and they spread them out one next to the other on her bed. Nicholas set the box down on top of the papers and admired the treasure. Lucy sat down beside the box and he opposite her. He hesitated before picking the box back up again, not wanting to spoil the moment. Lucy obviously wanted him to do the honors.

Finally when the tension proved too much, Nicholas picked up the box and placed the tips of his thumbs just beneath the bottom of the lid. He pushed once, but nothing happened. He pushed again, this time with a little more force, but still nothing. He could feel his face getting red with embarrassment as he looked to Lucy. The humor in her eyes told him that she saw his awkwardness. It took a stronger push than he would have imagined, breaking the box lid free, but it finally gave way with a squeak of the two rusty hinges and rose straight up. A long rolled up piece of paper that looked like a scroll, yellowed with age, rested in the box.

"I wonder what it says," Nicholas said with a tremor of fear in his voice. Lucy gave him a soothing look, one of her reminders that everything was on track. She clearly waited for his lead. He lifted the fragile and brittle roll of paper from the box and slid off the bed down to the floor on his knees. Slowly, with the utmost care, he unrolled the scroll an inch at a time until it was fully opened, then laid it out flat on the smooth blue bed spread before them.

Elation warmed him as he started to read from the paper, the large handwritten script. "Earth Champion," he began. There was that title again. He looked up at Lucy, who watched without blinking like a wise old owl. Her expression baffled him. What did she know that he didn't?

He continued reading in the most even of tones he could muster. "Your concern for the Earth will guide your way home. Stay true to your path and the Guides will be with you.

That was all it said. A wide range of emotions swept over him, gratitude, and then sadness that became insecurity. Maybe talking to the spirits wasn't such a good idea. His doubt quickly turned to hope as the seconds ticked away and he looked at Lucy. Her warmth and confidence in him gave him strength. The discovery of the scroll was just the beginning of something much greater.

CHAPTER THIRTEEN

The candle flickered, then became still. Nicholas squirmed about on the top of the picnic cooler. Lucy and he had gathered in the pantry to speak with Ruben and his teacher Abraxas, but Nicholas just couldn't concentrate. He held Lucy's hands, watching her and trying not to disturb her as he shifted again. She looked absorbed in meditation, her eyes closed, and her face aglow. Nicholas felt a slight breeze on his face as the flame of the candle between them on the rough board table flickered again. Ruben's words came back to him. "At the back of the wind lies a secret place." "Lucy," he whispered, not wanting to disturb her. Lucy didn't flinch. Lucy," he said, a little louder. The concentration lines on Lucy's forehead disappeared as she relaxed her face and slowly opened her eyes

"Nicholas," she whispered.

Nicholas chuckled. They didn't need to be quiet. Nobody was in the house except Lucy and him. "I forgot to tell you something," he said squeezing her hands.

"What's that?" she whispered back.

"Ruben told me something else when we were here last time.

"What's that?" she whispered again, giving a mischievous grin.

Nicholas enjoyed her response. "He said at the back of the wind lies a secret place.

Lucy bugged her eyes out and looked straight up at the ceiling, then down to her left and back to her right as if searching for something.

"I think I know what he meant," Nicholas said, trying to keep a straight face.

"What's that?" Lucy whispered playfully, her eyes still wide and her mouth hanging open.

Nicholas chuckled. "Well. He paused for a moment. "If you don't want to know… He looked down at the candle flame, then back at Lucy.

"You think there's a wind in here?" Lucy asked, looking serious.

"Well," Nicholas said. "It can't be coming from the kitchen unless it's coming in under the door. He swung his left leg over the board they sat on and stood up, then bent over and held his hand in front of the crack beneath the door. "Nope, nada, there's no air coming in from down here.

He straightened up and looked about. There weren't any windows in the room, just three bare stucco walls and another wall of shelves filled with quart jars of canned food. The cool damp air smelled musty. Nicholas shivered and rubbed the goose bumps on his arms. He shouldn't have worn short sleeves.

Standing quite still and fully aware that Lucy didn't move, he stared at the candle flame. It was still at first, but then he felt a slight gust of wind coming from his left and the candle slowly began to waver.

"It's a wind," Lucy whispered. "It has to be. We're not moving.

Nicholas looked at the shelves where the quart jars gleamed in the candle light. He could see behind the jars of peaches and pears to the wooden back of the shelves. The old unpainted boards still fit tightly together, but just above a shelf of green bean jars, he noticed a knothole about the size of a quarter. He held the candle flame up level with the knothole.

"I don't see how any wind could get in this place from there, Nicholas," Lucy said, getting up. "This pantry was dug way back into the side of the hill. There couldn't be anything back there except dirt.

"We'll see," Nicholas said. "Let's be really still. I really thought I felt a breeze blowing from this direction.

Two metal crossbars, attached to the face of the shelves, appeared to give them support. The bars formed an x. In the center of the x, a large metal bolt attached the bars to a vertical iron rod that ran from the ceiling to the floor and passed through each shelf. The crossbars and vertical rod looked too thick and strong for the old shelves. They wouldn't need that much bracing.

The candle flame flickered. Nicholas felt the breeze again, just barely.

"Give me a hand, will you?" he asked, setting the candle on a shelf before them. "Let's get a better look at these shelves. Let's move this table and everything.

"Oh sure," Lucy said, "just when I was making contact with the spirits too.

"You were?" he asked, picking up one end of the board table.

Lucy picked up the other end of the board. "No, not really. I just like razzing you.

Nicholas laughed and shook his head from side to side as they leaned the board against one wall. Lucy started to roll the barrel away from the shelves, but Nicholas intentionally bumped her rump with his and knocked her playfully to one side.

"I'll move this if you please," he said snatching the barrel away from her and spinning it away from the shelves. Hey," she said. "What's the big idea?"

Nicholas set the barrel against the wall, then bent over and reached for the picnic cooler. Lucy tickled him under his arms and he jumped, slapping his arms closed to protect himself, but too late. She reached around his chest and hugged him close. He reeled with the sensation of her warmth against his back, not wanting to pull away.

"I'm sorry," he said, touching the smooth skin of her arms. "I didn't mean to be so mean.

"Oh, Nicholas, you could never be mean, not to me. She loosened her grip just enough for him to turn about and face her. He put his arms around her and looked into her eyes, shining in the candlelight. He'd never been this close to a girl before. His mom had hugged him before, but this was different. What should he do?

Lucy moved in closer, brushing his cheek with her own. He returned her hug gladly, letting himself go. She was so sweet and he found her nearness comforting. Just as they pulled back away from each other some, Lucy leaned toward him and kissed him full on the lips. The sudden explosion of desire that raced through his body made him fumble backwards a step. Oh my God, they had kissed!

He turned to face the shelves and stuck his thumbs in his back pockets. With his eyes squinted, he tried to look studious. He tried to slow his breathing, very much aware of his pounding heart. Things surely could change quickly on you sometimes. He hadn't really expected the kiss, but he couldn't say that he wanted to avoid it either, well, not too much anyway. He would love to do it again, but he didn't know how it had happened the first time, let alone how to repeat it.

"Do you suppose the wind's coming from behind these shelves?" he asked in a wavering voice, feeling like an idiot. Maybe he should try to kiss her again, but he wasn't sure she wanted him to. We could look and see, I guess," Lucy said confidently, her voice sounding deep and rich. The kiss had only seemed to make her more comfortable.

Nicholas wanted to look at her and tell her that he cared for her or something. He wasn't sure just what to say at such a time.

"Let's try moving the shelves away from the wall," he said.

He leaned over and tried to edge his fingers in between the shelves and the wall to pry them apart

"We'll have to pull on the front of the shelves," he said. "I can't get my fingers in here. Lucy leaned down beside him and together they pulled on the front of the shelf. The shelves moved an inch at a time, sliding slowly across the linoleum floor. Lucy started to grunt, and then groaned loudly. Nicholas laughed and stopped pulling on the shelves. He knew that Lucy was only joking. She stopped pulling too. Nicholas could only guess what her face must look like in the dim light. She was probably smiling.

"Pretty heavy uh?" he asked.

"Oh, we can do it if we keep trying," she said.

Nicholas stuck his right hand in the small gap between the shelves and the wall and wiggled his fingers. The gap seemed to go back farther than the wall itself. He brought out his right hand and stuck in his left, this time able to feel even more empty space where the wall should have been.

"You want to try again?" Lucy asked.

"Okay, but this time no moaning like a sick cow," Nicholas said. Her face was so close to his, but he could feel her more than see her.

"No promises," Lucy said. She leaned back down and grabbed the shelves.

Once more, they both pulled hard, sliding the shelves back several more inches from the wall. After they stopped, Nicholas put his hand back into the empty space behind the shelf where the wall should have been and moved his arm about. There must be a huge hole back there!

He stood up and walked behind Lucy to the front of the shelves. Just as he picked up the candle in its holder, he noticed a gap between the shelves and the wall on his left. There shouldn't be a gap there. The shelves must be swiveling about on the metal rod that ran down through them.

He took two steps toward the gap and held the candle up into it, then moved the candle back and forth in the empty space. It appeared to go back a long ways, but the closeness and brightness of the candle blinded him. His arm fit easily back into the gap, but his body wouldn't. He wedged himself as far in between the wall and the shelves as he could and pushed on the shelves with his back.

The shelves moved easily this time, sliding back even more into the dark space. He walked freely into it, holding the candle as high and far away as he could. As his eyes adjusted, he was amazed. He had found someone's secret place, a whole room dug back far into the Earth.

"Lucy," Nicholas said, his voice echoing, "look. He had discovered something so special, something that had been lost for many years, unseen by anyone.

A long rectangular table, with at least a dozen high backed wooden chairs set neatly around it, occupied the center of the large room.

"Whoa," Lucy said as she joined Nicholas by his side. "I didn't know this was back here. I bet no one does.

"Except us," Nicholas added. He started walking toward a corner of the room, shielding his eyes from the candle flame with his free hand. Lucy walked with him, their footsteps clicking on the plank floor. Several round wooden posts held up long wooden roof beams. Two by six rafters held up the ceiling. Long thin boards finished the ceiling and the walls, which shone with a surprising brilliance when Nicholas took a swipe at one. Someone had paid the greatest of attention in making the room. It looked as if it could easily last for another hundred years.

All four corners of the room proved empty. Lucy and Nicholas returned to the table and stared spellbound. A large dust covered book lay there on top of it. Maybe they had missed seeing the book before or it had never been there until now. Nicholas wasn't sure. He felt weak in the knees. A profound silence came over him. This book could change his life forever.

CHAPTER FOURTEEN

In his dream, the last breath Nicholas took filled him with such promise, but he couldn't recall what happened immediately after that. He flew through outer space as he watched the blue globe of the Earth becoming smaller and smaller beneath him. He was headed for the stars. Now he would be free of the Earth's pull, free to go wherever he wanted. What a wonderful feeling! Then something strange and totally unexpected happened.

Some unseen force pulled him down, back to the Earth, tugging upon his will. Then he saw them, a small group of bald-headed Asian men with dark skin and orange colored robes standing about on a flat grassy plain. They looked up at him and pulled him in with their minds like fishermen reeling in a fish.

Nicholas didn't really mind. What did the monks want? He found their sudden appearance a pleasant addition to his dream adventure. That's right. He was dreaming! What a way to find out things. The monks gathered about him as he landed on the Earth, their smiling faces bright with wisdom and a clean confidence.

In his mind, Nicholas heard the thoughts of one of the monks. "You can't leave yet.

"Why not?" Nicholas mentally asked.

"There is one lesson you must learn first," the monk replied.

"What is that?" Nicholas asked.

"Compassion," the monk replied. The word washed over Nicholas like healing waters from a spring. He felt compassion center in the pit of his stomach. The full meaning would only come with time. His life on Earth wasn't over yet. He had to complete this lesson, compassion. There was no doubt. Though he didn't know how it would come, he knew that it would finally free him. He'd heard the word compassion in church many times, but never until now had he felt so strongly about it.

This life of his was a personal quest to achieve something far beyond anything personal. His universe had to be seen in a new light now. His destiny would be like diving into the healing waters and floating, letting himself go completely, giving in to the feelings that carried him, without a single thought for himself.

Nicholas awoke the next morning and opened his eyes. His room looked brilliant with sunlight streaming in through his window, illuminating his erector set skyscrapers on his desk. To learn compassion was his lesson in life. What a strange but beautiful idea. It meant so much and was such a tall order, yet it gave him something to cling to. To learn compassion would be another adventure, larger and more fantastic than all the ones before it. That journey would take him beyond his wildest dreams.

He couldn't help feeling that the dusty old book from the secret room had something to do with the monks in his dream and his newfound destiny. The first time he saw the book, he knew it would change his life. Nicholas called up the memory of finding the book and let it play forward like a movie, reliving every moment from the night before, clearly envisioning the book as Lucy and he had found it the night before on the big oak table.

"What do you think it is?" Lucy asked in his memory.

"Probably a journal," he replied without thinking.

Nicholas approached the book with fear as well as with hopeful anticipation. It looked untouched, its thick layer of dust perfectly matching the dusty table. It would have been easy to overlook the book when Lucy and he had first entered the room. But Nicholas felt foolish, as if he just wasn't quite with the program. There were so many things in life he didn't understand.

The book challenged him. He just stood there, not wanting to pick it up, but afraid not to. Lucy stepped forward and picked up the book. She held it close to the candle light and brushed the dusty cover with her hand. Six shafts of golden ripe grain, bearing three cup-shaped white flowers graced the cover. Beneath the strange but beautiful plant was a huge silver "O."

His interest in the book lay deep inside him, a private place where he kept things he longed to share with others, a soft and tender spot that he had protected for so long. Lucy looked to Nicholas as if for permission then opened the book to its middle. As she stared at the page and Nicholas breathed in the dust flying about in the air, he thought he could pass out. Never had he felt so drawn and repelled by anything at the same time.

His breath caught in his throat, a fearful choking that unnerved him. Then as if he were outside of his body and looking down at it, he saw the smallness of his hesitation. He was afraid, but he knew it to be a silly reaction, one that he couldn't totally control.

He would shut away as much of his fear in the back of his mind where he would review it later. He would label it "Paranoia" and file it under the category of "Most Likely Ridiculous." It was funny how one's mind worked. Even with his fear, he could still look ahead, knowing that he would have to read every last page of the book that Lucy so comfortably held open faced in her hands.

"What do you think?" he managed to spit out, the words sticking to his dry tongue. He swallowed once to moisten the inside of his mouth as he watched Lucy devour the page with her eyes.

Finally she looked up from the book. "Nicholas, you have to read this. It's fantastic."

Nicholas saw a sudden flash of purple light around Lucy's head and shoulders. It must be her aura. He had read that every person has an electromagnetic field around him or her. Man, she must be electric! Either the book had affected her and or he was beginning to see energy more than ever. He liked the last idea, but he also felt like a scared old man, a fuddy dud, somebody afraid of his own shadow, that hard to grasp part of themselves they know hides the truth.

"I'll read it later," he said. "You take it with you. I have to go." Once the reluctant words came out of his mouth, Nicholas regretted them. He was digging himself deeper and deeper into a hole all because he was afraid of the unknown. Tyco would never have let him hear the last of such nonsense. Nicholas was afraid just because Lucy and he had found a secret room and an old book. But it was so much more than that. He told himself he would return to his old confident self once the edge of his fear wore off and he had a chance to distance himself from it. The room seemed to be spinning. He had to get out of there quickly.

The memories of the secret room still lived in Nicholas as he watched the sun reflecting off the erector set buildings on top of the desk in his bedroom. He always imagined the skyscrapers to be a part of New York City. He felt safe lying in his bed, knowing that nothing could hurt him. He figured that the only thing that could ever really hurt him would be caused by his own thoughts. Other than his body being maimed or crippled by some unseen attacker or accident there was really nothing to worry about. He told himself that over and over as he got up from bed and dressed. He had nothing to be afraid of.

Just why was he so afraid? That question turned in his head as he tromped downstairs and found his mother sitting in her favorite spot on the sofa, hemming a pair of his pants. Her hands moved with precision and fluidity, her nimble fingers threading the needle like an archer would notch an arrow to her bow. He draped himself over the arm of the couch with his legs crossed, the full weight of his body resting precariously on one hip. With one hand, he pressed against the back of the couch, balancing himself in place. He loved to put his body in the most unusual and exotic positions just to see if he could and to see if his mother would notice. Sometimes she did, but usually like now she was too distracted to care.

"What's for breakfast," he asked feeling impish.

"Well, there's some cracked wheat still warm in the pan," she said without looking up from her work. "If it is cold, you'll have to warm it up. Your dad and I ate quite a while ago, but there are some ripe bananas you can cut up into it if you want."

Nicholas got up from the couch, knowing that his mom was in no mood for fun. She was too serious most of the time. On his way to the kitchen, he thought about the old Dragnet television series. One show completely cracked him up. The main character, a detective with the driest of dry personalities, stood on a lady's front porch and questioned her as she leaned out the door. She avoided the detective's eyes as she answered, complaining about her son's trouble finding a job.

"Just the facts, ma'am," the detective said, looking up at her with a stone-cold expression, holding his pencil ready to record answers that weren't forthcoming.

Out in the kitchen, Nicholas got out a big wooden spoon from a top counter drawer and doled out a huge glob of cereal from the metal pan on the stove into his glass bowl on the counter. "Just the facts," he said doing the dance he had seen Tyco do. He spun about once and tossed the spoon back into the pan where it stuck in the gooey mass with a plop. "Just the facts," he said again, sitting down at the table and pouring milk from a pitcher all over his cereal.

CHAPTER FIFTEEN

Strips of lavender ribbon tied in bows at the ends of Lucy's pigtails made her look kind of silly, she thought. She sat before her dresser and studied herself in the mirror. Maybe if she squinted her eyes the wrinkles at the corners would make her look older. It did a little, but she still looked silly with the pigtails. She had braided her hair that morning, taking only a few minutes, sitting at the dresser in her long pink nightgown.

The old book from the secret room behind the pantry lay on her green silk scarf spread out on the high chest of drawers. She hadn't read the book yet, nor did she intend to. When she and Nicholas had first found the book the night before, she had marveled at the intricacy and depth of the surprising descriptions she read, something about the ancient history of the Earth 500,000 years ago.

This morning's look into the book had shocked her completely. She had opened it to the first page inside the front cover and read the handwritten script in awe: "For The Earth Champion." The book was obviously meant for Nicholas to read. Both Ruben and Abraxas had called Nicholas the Earth Champion.

Lucy scrunched up her nose and slowly wiggled her ears, watching herself in the mirror. She had made the pigtails for Nicholas. He might be the Earth Champion (whatever that was) furthermore; he was terribly cute for a younger guy. The pigtails would probably make him laugh, something not so hard to do. She could practically do it any time she wished.

The old book bothered her. She needed to do something with it. It belonged in Nicholas' hands, but he had reacted so weirdly to it. She wished he could read the book.

She got up from her dresser and walked over to her chest of drawers. The old book was still in pretty good shape except for one frayed corner. The picture on the hard cloth cover intrigued her. It portrayed the strangest of plants with three large cup shaped flowers on several stalks of ripe grain. The book must contain such wonders. Lucy had agreed to meet Nicholas at the corner up the street a block, so they could walk downtown. Feelings of joy that she felt for Nicholas blossomed inside her. She would see him soon.

She walked back over in front of her mirror and cringed. She had forgotten that Nicholas was moving away soon. Her face suddenly turned white, filled with despair. She wanted to rip out the ribbons and pull out all her hair. Why, oh why did Nicholas have to leave?

Lucy pranced up the sidewalk toward Nicholas who stood near the corner. To Nicholas she looked like a Catholic schoolgirl in her short plaid skirt and outrageous pigtails. He couldn't keep a straight face. He wrapped his arms around himself and bent over to hold in the laughter. Several chuckles tried to escape as she approached, but he clenched his teeth and held them in. Then he saw that Lucy didn't mind, so he let it all go, laughing as if his life depended on it. Lucy seemed to be enjoying the show. She looked immensely pleased with herself.

Once his fit of laughter died down, Lucy turned her head from side to side like a model showing off. She batted her eyelashes and said, "I hope you like my new pigtails?"

She was such a good sport and too funny to believe.

"Yeah, I love them," he said and burst out laughing again. He didn't know where the laughter came from, but he couldn't stop. He fell on the ground beside the sidewalk and rolled onto his stomach, letting the grass absorb spasm after spasm.

Finally he got up and brushed himself off with no harm done. Boy, Lucy was crazy. She had dressed up like that on purpose, just to make him laugh. He knew it. She might also want him to think that if she wore braids she wasn't too old for him.

"My, my," Lucy said as they began to walk. "You sure are the wacko."

Nicholas chuckled and smiled. "You should talk. Just look at the way you're dressed."

Lucy looked down at her patent leather shoes and long white stockings, and then turned around as far as she could to inspect her backside. "What do you mean?" she asked.

"Your pigtails, goofball."

"Don't you like them?"

"Sure, but they are kinda."

"Wacko?" Lucy asked.

"Yeah, wacko," Nicholas replied.

"Oh, well, that makes two of us."

They started walking up the street. Their meeting almost seemed like a date or something. Nicholas had never had a date before, but this surely would pass as one. The whole idea of dates seemed kind of stupid, but he enjoyed strolling along.

"Where do you want to go first?"

"I don't care," Lucy replied. "Let's just see where we end up.

"You want to see the old ice house that burned down last winter?" he asked.

"No thanks," Lucy said with a smile. "My father took me to see it already."

"How about the grain elevator? There are some great pigeons that live up in the top of it."

"I thought you wanted to go downtown?"

"I do, but there are so many cool places."

"We could get some ice cream," Lucy offered.

"Hmm, that sounds good. What's your favorite?"

"Peach."

"Mine's chocolate chip."

"Nicholas, do you think the spirits are watching us?"

"They must be. There must be gobs of them."

"I always think about that," Lucy said. "You never hear people talk about it much. I mean after everyone dies there must be a lot of them hanging around."

Nicholas watched the houses and the streets lined with tall elm trees thick with green leaves fluttering in the wind. Everything they passed, the cars, the people, and the fresh smell of summer in the air, all made him a little sad. He would be leaving Flat Rock for good. The town had not been unkind to him. He would miss it.

"I think everyone thinks that people all go to heaven when they die," Nicholas said, "and that's that."

"Heaven," Lucy said disgusted. "Everyone pretends that heaven is this magic wand you wave over somebody when they die and everything is hunky dory after that. I wish it would be that simple. I mean in some ways, maybe it is, but I don't believe it's quite like that, do you?"

Hunky dory had a nice ring. "Maybe," he replied, "but I doubt it. I think most people can get away with being bad in this life, but you know what the Bible says."

"What's that?" Lucy asked, licking her lips in a delightful way.

"As you sow, so shall you reap," he said, looking up at the sky.

"Yeah, that's what I mean, Nicholas. I don't think you can get away with being bad. It'll catch up with you eventually. We'll have to take it up with Abraxas or my Grandpa. Maybe they could tell us more."

Without checking the traffic, Lucy took a step out into Main Street. They were in the cross-walk at a four-way stop on the corner of Main Street and Fleming. Nicholas knew there was no danger, but he suddenly reached out and pressed his hand to the base of her throat, forcing her to stop.

"Oh my God," he said, "I just saved your life."

Lucy blushed. "More like broke my neck," she said, smiling. They started walking again as if nothing had happened.

"Don't you think spirits are neat, Nicholas?" Lucy asked, sounding unsure.

"I guess so he replied, glad to be talking about anything. "Yeah, sure they are."

"Why do you think we found that coin and the little wooden box Ruben told us about?" she asked.

"I think it was like a test, to see if we could follow instructions."

"How about the room behind the pantry?"

As they passed the grocery store, Nicholas looked through the big plate glass window. You never knew who might be inside.

"I was thinking about that," he said. "Don't you think your Granddad used it to hide those slaves you told me about, you know like in the Underground Railroad?"

"Yeah, you're probably right," Lucy said excited.

"And maybe they held those séances there too," Nicholas added.

A lush crop of wild sunflowers, growing in the vacant lot beside the sidewalk looked so inviting. Nicholas picked one as they passed, saying thank you silently to the flower as he did so and handed it to Lucy. She accepted it graciously and held it with both hands before her. He would have loved the moment to last forever, but it slipped away. He felt sad again. His closeness with Lucy would soon change when he and his family moved.

"There are not a lot of people who think spirits can help us," he said feeling shaky. "They think that spirits are silly or scary or that they don't even exist. Most people certainly don't think spirits can help us."

"That's true, Nicholas. You know Tyco said we would see each other again after you left."

Nicholas perked up. "I guess people think the spirits might interfere with Gods plan or something," he said, "you know, like we won't listen to God or something."

"Maybe some spirits can help us do that," Lucy said. She stuck the flower behind her ear and gave him a loving look.

Nicholas felt courageous. "You're the greatest, Lucy!" he blurted, taking her right hand in his left.

Next to the sidewalk, the field of sunflowers swayed in the breeze, their golden faces a joyful witness of his happiness. He tripped on a bump in the sidewalk and stumbled forward, letting loose of Lucy's hand. Feeling foolish, he ran to the end of the block where he stood by a tall wooden board fence. Lucy approached slowly. He turned, placed his hands on her shoulders, looked solidly into her eyes and said, "Promise me one thing, Lucy." She looked as serious as he felt.

"Don't ever forget that we're friends," he said and released her.

They walked across the street and into Mulligan's ice cream store. Nicholas held the door for Lucy, feeling older than his 12 years. Although they were doing what most kids would love to do, getting ice cream, he didn't feel quite as young as he had. He felt something click inside him as it rolled into place; an emotional cog clicked into place and sealed itself, giving him new strength. He really did have a friend in Lucy. Her comforting presence said far more than words.

They bought two Styrofoam bowls of ice cream and sat down at opposite sides of a pink plastic table near the front window. The stores candy colored walls, hot pink and brilliant purple, reminded him of the bubble gum pink stream and the rolling purple hills they had so joyfully walked past on their way to Oberon. What a grand dream that was!

A long silver mirror behind the ice cream counter made the inside of the store look huge. Two rows of padded pink plastic booths that filled the store were empty. Lucy and he had the place to themselves, except for the ice cream guy who stood behind the counter.

The pale young man looked bored and tired, drooping in his baggy white uniform. His bushy red hair bulged out from beneath a small white hat that clung tightly to his skull like moss on a rock. Nicholas decided to send some of his own happiness out to the man, something that seemed to have instant effect. The young man started wiping at the glass counter with a dishrag as if he suddenly loved his job. Tyco had told Lucy and Nicholas that you could change the world around you, change things with your thoughts.

After a while, the young man smiled timidly at Nicholas and picked up a pencil and notebook beside the cash register. He flipped through the pages with interest and began writing.

Lucy looked happy too. With melted peach ice cream smeared on her lips, she ate with abandonment. Nicholas sucked the ice cream away from the bunch of chocolate chips he had saved up in his mouth and chewed them slowly. Lucy could be so entertaining, like watching cartoons.

She pulled loose the bow from one of her pigtails and unbraided her hair, then tilted back her head and shook it from side to side. Her long black hair flopped about her face and whacked her in the throat. She gargled melted ice cream as she continued to shake her head. Finally she stopped her shenanigans and closed her eyes. Her stony features told no story.

Nicholas waited, absorbed in her show. She looked like a true cartoon character now with half her hair frizzed out on one side. She partially opened one eye and stared at him through the slit.

Nicholas swallowed the chewed up mass of chocolate chips and reached for his bowl like one in a daze. With her crazy hair do, Lucy looked like some strange exotic jungle bird. Her lips glistened and were pressed tightly together as she gripped the table top with both hands and closed her eye.

Nicholas scooped out a spoonful of ice cream and brought it up for a bite. Just as he opened his mouth, Lucy lunged forward across the table; her eyes still closed and gulped it down. Man, this girl had talent! She could see with her eyes closed.

Lucy sat straight up, eyes still closed as Nicholas dipped back into his bowl of ice cream with his spoon. As he raised it slowly, the melted ice cream dripping down into his bowl, he opened his mouth wide. Lucy lunged forward, clamping down on the plastic spoon with her teeth. Her eyes sprang open then like she had just come to life as she sucked the ice cream with a slurp. Nicholas couldn't help but laugh deep tremors that shook him all the way down in this belly. This girl was tops! Finally he stopped laughing. "Man, you're a wacko," he said, "a real wacko. Do you know any other tricks?"

"Nope," Lucy replied, her hair still askew, "fresh out."

"Yes, well that's just peachy," he said. "I can't imagine what you'll do next. Maybe we'll have a pig scramble."

Lucy fingered her only pigtail and batted her eyelashes at him. "Shoot," she said. "You sure know how to sweet talk a girl."

Between his attraction for Lucy and his buzz from the ice cream, Nicholas felt like he was floating up toward the ceiling. He grabbed the edges of the table to steady his self and looked about the store.

"Do you really think we'll see each other after I leave?" he asked, avoiding her eyes.

Lucy placed her hands over his. "I hope so," she said quietly. "We have to. There's no other way. We just have to. We could dream about each other you know."

"Yeah," Nicholas said, "like last time. Maybe when we're old and gray we'll sit around in wheel chairs and sing songs or something. You never know. Maybe we'll still like each other then."

"Oh, I wouldn't go that far," Lucy said, pretending to be angry. She stood up as if to leave, then reconsidering, sat back down. She hadn't fooled Nicholas. He knew she was playing a game. He too stood up as if to leave, giving her the most somber look as he pushed in his chair beneath the table. He paused for a moment, then pulled the chair back out and sat down. They stared each other down.

Though it appeared that she was trying to hide it, Nicholas felt that Lucy would miss him. She might be sad when he left, but she would be more than all right. She had too much life in her. As the tension mounted between them, they both burst out laughing at the same time. Their fun together would always outweigh anything bad that might try to come between them.

"Boy, will I miss your ugly face," he said, leaning back in his chair till the front legs came up off the floor. Lucy reached over and slapped him on the arm. Nicholas grabbed the edge of the table and pulled himself back down to place, all four chair legs squarely on the floor. Then he reached forward and swatted Lucy on her bare arm in return. "I bet you can't figure out what I'm thinking," he said, crossing his arms and glaring at her.

Lucy looked stern. She stood up, leaned forward, and kissed him on the cheek. "That's what," she said, and then walked over to the door, pushed it open, and walked out.

After he got over the shock, Nicholas jumped up from his chair and headed for the door. Lucy had known his thoughts without even trying! She had known that he was thinking that he liked her a lot. Man, life would be so simple if everyone could read each other's thoughts. It didn't take long for him to catch up to her outside on the sidewalk. Main Street looked dead as usual. The plain brick buildings seemed so ordinary, nothing like the large cities Nicholas had seen on television.

An old man with a cane walked on the opposite side of the street. The old man paused momentarily to get his bearings, and then looked up with great interest at a big blue Cadillac that went slowly by. The little old lady who drove the car sat low in her seat, peering over the steering wheel with a worried look as if she had never driven before.

The lady and her boat of a car would be swept away by traffic in a larger town. A simple and sleepy place, Flat Rock had captured everyone in a sleeping spell. Nicholas felt protected and safe there, but something was missing. What would moving be like?

After walking for a block, Lucy and he entered the used bookstore. It smelled like dust and musty old books. The bookshelves rose to the ceiling and were crammed with magazines, paperbacks, and books laying this way and that. Nicholas liked the disorganized place. He found his way to a section of tattered paperbacks. Jammed between a stack of photography books and a stack of engine manuals, he spotted a copy of a Funk and Wagnall's dictionary. He picked it up and thumbed through it while Lucy wandered off in another direction.

First, he looked up the word "Tara", but found no listing. He had forgotten that "Tara" was probably an Italian or Latin word. He looked up "champion"--the holder of first place in a contest, one who defends another person. Hmm, if Tara meant Earth, he would be a defender of the Earth. Earth Champion was a nice title, but it made him feel silly. Such a big job would be only given to someone pure and wise. Surely that wouldn't be him. His thoughts often turned sour at the worst times and he lacked confidence when it mattered most. He liked the sound of Earth Champion. Maybe he could make defending the Earth his life's mission. "Mission", now there was a word. He looked it up in the dictionary. "Mission"--an assignment or task to be carried out. Nicholas already knew the general meaning of mission, but words fascinated him. He loved to know their specific meanings and how they came about.

Right beneath "mission," he saw the word "missionary"--a person sent to do religious or charitable work, usually in a foreign country. Now that would be something. The monk in his dream had told him he needed to learn compassion. Thumbing backwards he found the word "compassion"--sympathy for someone who is suffering or distressed in some way. Compassion was a hard one sometimes. There were days when he just wanted to ignore people even though he knew they were hurting. Anyway, it seemed a lot of people wanted to bite your hand when you did offer to help them. But then maybe you could still feel compassion for them. He certainly felt compassion for the Earth, but that seemed easy. The Earth never hurt anyone intentionally.

Down the aisle, he spotted Lucy leaning sideways against a wall plastered with a bunch of childlike crayon drawings. She studied a large white book that she held open in her hands. Nicholas walked up beside her and looked over her shoulder. A picture of a high desert mesa filled a whole page in her book. An old adobe Indian village stood on top the beautiful mesa, the earth browns, reds, and yellow all blending together, making it appear to grow right out of the rocky landscape. He would love to live there.

Nicholas felt pulled to walk farther up the aisle away from Lucy to a section of old hardback books stacked straight up on edge. His nose began to itch as he scanned the titles one by one. He scratched his nose with his finger once, and then wiggled when the itch wouldn't go away. His nose rarely did this. The itch seemed out of place. Maybe it wasn't, though. Maybe he was tuning into something.

Scanning the books made him feel calm and that he belonged, exactly where he stood in the store. Like the adobe village, he belonged on this very spot. Nothing else mattered, but his search, looking without expectation.

His eyes fixed on a black hardback book with no visible title. The book seemed out of place. He pulled it out from the shelf and gasped, his jaw dropping in disbelief. On the book cover was three cup-shaped white flowers on stalks of ripened grain. Beneath that was a large silver "O". The book looked exactly like the one Lucy and he had found in the secret room behind the pantry. It could be a copy.

His nose itched even more now, a painless sensation that seemed to react to the book. He opened the book to the middle. The words printed on the page were so small that he couldn't read them. He had good eyes, 20/20 in fact, but these tiny words must be made for insects to read. He squinted his eyes as he moved the book closer, then farther away. Strange, he still couldn't read a word. A magnifying glass would be handy about now. His nose stopped itching.

He flipped through several pages in the book, but they were all blank. The two pages with the tiny print had disappeared. This was stranger than strange. After flipping through every page in the book several times, forward and backwards without finding anything but blank pages, he gave up. Man, this was bizarre! Lucy would get a kick out of this.

She stood in the same place, reading the same white book on Indians when he approached her. "Look what I found," he said.

Lucy looked surprised when she saw the book in his hands. She put hers down flat on a middle shelf and took his. Nicholas" nose began to itch again.

"This is just like the one we found behind the pantry, Nicholas!" she exclaimed. "I know. I just looked at it again this morning before we came here. See this damaged corner where the binding's frayed. The book we found is just like this one. I really think you are supposed to read it, Nicholas." She looked excited and concerned.

"I tried to just now," he said feeling foolish, "but take a look and you'll see why I can't."

Lucy opened the book to two pages of full-sized writing.

Nicholas could see the writing, though from his position opposite her, he couldn't read upside down. A peculiar wave of heat smacked him in the face and spread throughout his whole body. He panicked. Suddenly the store had become the last place he wanted to be, but Lucy's presence held him there. Something about the book had upset him, but he didn't know what. He felt like a scared four year old. The room started to spin. He felt dizzy. His throat was dry. His eyes watered with tears.

Lucy put her hand on his shoulder. The spinning room slowed and he started to regain his balance. What had happened?

Lucy handed him his book, which he received, feeling estranged. A tingling sensation, pleasant and cooling, came over him. Man, life was weird!

"You looked pretty bad there for a second," Lucy said, "but you look okay now. What happened?"

"I don't know really," he replied, "must be something I ate. He gave Lucy a wooden grin and wiped his forehead with one of his short sleeves. Then he wiped his mouth and nose with his other sleeve, smelling the fresh scent of clean laundry. His mother would consider him crazy if she knew about all of the things that kept happening to him. There was something about that book.

"I really do feel that we should get this book for you," Lucy said. "I have plenty of money if you need some.

"But you already have this book at home," Nicholas said.

"I know, Lucy said, "but I'll get this one for you as a present. I have a feeling about it."

Maybe he should open the book again to see if he could find any writing, just to see. No, he would go along with Lucy's offer. Okay," he said, feeling confused. Lucy had that look of certainty that he wanted to trust.

CHAPTER SIXTEEN

Nicholas awoke with music playing in his head. Hundreds of tiny bells tinkled along with the accompaniment of deep drums beating a sober rhythm. The song reminded him of Tyco and his troupe of dwarves. Where was Tyco? Would he ever see him again?

Lying in his bed half awake and half asleep, he realized that the music came from beside him. He turned onto his side and opened his eyes. The sounds seemed to be right next to him, as close to him as his nightstand. How could that be?

He stared at the book lying on his nightstand next to his clock. The cloth book cover gave off a pale pink light, so strange and beautiful. The music changed then. Deep male voices sang a hypnotic chant without any accompaniment. The chanting made him feel warm inside in a way that reminded him of the silken amber creature.

Nicholas listened, receiving the music that filled him. If he tried to figure out what was happening, the music might stop. The pink light began to fade and he knew that he had caused it. The music faded as well. It was hard not to think, hard not to let the mind take control. As he reached for the book, he could still hear the chant, but it seemed to only come from within his head now. He opened the book near the front, pleased to see two full pages of writing that he could actually read. The heading took up the first three lines.

THE ART OF SUFFERING AND THE PAIN OF REALITY IN THE TWELVE DIMENSIONS OF LEARNING

Wow, that sounded heavy. He started to read the first paragraph beneath the heading.

"Imagine you are the soul of another being and follow the threads of the time space continuum."

Whew, the writing sounded so serious, but what did it mean? He would have to think about it.

The writing on both pages began to fade. Thinking could be destructive. He had made the writing disappear. He would have loved to read on, but that wouldn't be possible, at least not now. He swallowed once, feeling that he had just taken a huge dose of some crazy medicine. This book was so...

A knock at his bedroom door broke his train of thought. It must be Lucy. She probably had some news.

"Come in," he said without moving.

The door opened just enough for Lucy to peek around it. She hesitated when she saw that he was still in bed.

"Come in. I won't bite."

She opened the door wide and stepped in.

"What's up?" Nicholas asked as she shut the door behind her.

"I see you found some light reading," she said smiling.

"I don't know how light it is, but this book is really something else!"

Lucy walked over and sat down beside him on the bed. She wore a red midi tank top and a short white skirt. Her thick hair was tied back in a ponytail.

"You wouldn't believe..."

"Yes I would," she interrupted. "Nicholas it's so fantastic. This is the same book we found behind the pantry."

"How do you know?" he asked, getting up on his elbow.

"Because mine's disappeared, only it's not mine. It's yours. You were supposed to read it."

Nicholas believed Lucy. If she said her book had disappeared then it had. Not only could his book play music, but also it could make words disappear and reappear. The book had probably appeared in the bookstore just for him. He felt queasy. A lump in his stomach grew heavy.

"I don't know why it's here," he said.

"Maybe it's here to help you," Lucy said. "You know you have a lot of questions."

"I know, but..."

"I know its strange Nicholas, but we won't tell anyone. It'll be our secret."

Nicholas liked the kind look in Lucy's eyes, but his stomach growled and started to hurt. Who would have thought that any of the strange events of the past few weeks would have happened? What was next? He felt a little out of his league. It sure felt hot in the room. The window was open, but he felt closed in.

"You want to look at this?" he asked holding the book out to her.

"I guess not. I think it's meant for you really."

"Yeah, I guess so. He lay the book down on the nightstand.

"I just stopped for a sec," Lucy said. "I have to get back home. My mom wants me to help her. I just wanted to tell you about the book. You do believe me don't you?"

Nicholas nodded without taking his eyes off the book.

"Okey dokey Smokey," she said, getting up. She walked over to the door and opened it. "See ya later." She swished out the door with a sway of her hips and closed the door behind her. The door opened again and Lucy stuck her head back in his room. "All right Charlie?"

Nicholas grinned and chuckled. "All right."

He started feeling really sick after Lucy left. His queasy stomach got worse and he started to get a fever. His nose ran, his eyes burned, his head ached, everything ached, his whole body, especially his joints. He knew why he was sick. The Book of O had been too much for him.

It was strange that the book had appeared in his life. The book's power was real, but somehow he felt that the power came from within him. Somehow the book magnified his energy and created its many special effects. At least that was the most likely explanation. Even so, who had ever heard of such a book? He didn't know where it came from or what exactly it was doing in his life, but he felt that it had come to help him. Oh yeah, he felt sick all right, sick like in monkey fever. That's what he always called it when he got sick, monkey fever.

Later that day, he had lunch with his mother downstairs in the kitchen. They sat across from each other at the Formica table, Nicholas plate filled with food that he would never be able to eat. His mother must think he was part horse. There were fried pork chops snow peas, mashed potatoes and gravy, and even a huge lop of leftover spaghetti. His mom knew he could never pass over spaghetti, but today was different.

"What's wrong Nicholas?" she asked.

"Nicholas wrapped his hand around his glass of milk. The coolness felt good to his hot hand.

"I have a bad case of monkey fever."

"You do?" His mother said as if it were a question, the ooh sound of her do going upward to the highest possible pitch, hurting his ears. She got up from her seat and walked over to him. Brushing away his unruly hair from his forehead, she placed her palm there.

Nicholas felt that all the energy in his whole body was being sucked right up out of him and into her hand. He felt weaker than ever before, so weak that he could just let his head fall right into his pile of mashed potatoes and gravy on his plate. He waited for his mother to pronounce sentence. This could be his last meal.

"Maybe we should take your temperature," she finally said.

Unbelievable! She had just felt his temperature with her hand and now she had to put a number on it. As if that would help! Oh, well, what was that saying he had heard in one of those World War Two movies, "resistance is futile." The bright lights up above, his mom's irritating high-pitched falsetto voice, and his unbearable weakness, all made him feel like a Nazi Gestapo agent was interrogating him.

"I'll be okay," he managed to spit out. "I just need to take it easy for a while." He couldn't ever remember getting sick in the summertime. Looking at his plate made him nauseous.

His mom brushed the lint off the hem of her red plaid dress as she asked, "Why don't you go up to your room and rest?

Oh no, another question. Then he realized that she hadn't meant for him to answer.

"I'll do the dishes," she said. Though his mother was only five feet tall in her shoes, she seemed to tower above him. He felt like he was shrinking down into himself, growing smaller as his stomach churned the greasy pork chops and gravy he had forced down. His mother reached for his glass of milk with a vacant look on her face. She had already forgotten him and couldn't wait to clear the table. Oh, life's chores. At least he wouldn't have to do any now. If only he could just make it upstairs.

When Nicholas stood up, his head spun with fever and his stomach lurched in several conflicting directions. His skin hung loose like an elephants. He felt so heavy that every step he took toward the stairs took forever.

Once he finally made it to the top of the steps, the carpeted hallway didn't feel real or steady beneath his feet. He headed for the bathroom feeling rotten, his stomach boiling a sickening brew. Just as he reached the doorway his stomach let loose, and heaved up its contents. Puke spewed out from his mouth and down to the linoleum floor with a plop plop. Whoa, what a rush!

Nicholas tiptoed through the juicy brown mess in his tennis shoes and grabbed the cold porcelain edge of the toilet bowl. With another sickening surge of his poor stomach, he heaved again, this time safely in the toilet bowl. Oh God, that must be the last one. He squatted there for a little, trying to get his bearings. It had been years since he'd puked up like that. Now he felt better. Luckily his mother hadn't heard him or she'd come running up the stairs to order him about. He had to clean up this mess before she saw it.

Nicholas pulled a big orange towel from the wall rack and started sponging up the putrid goo on the floor. The smell gagged him, but he wiped until the towel was full and sopping wet. Then he rinsed the towel out in the sink and wrung it out with a twist, using every ounce of strength he had left. It took quite a few times in his weakened state, but he finally cleaned not only the floor, but also the towel and the soles of his tennis shoes.

With his shoes in his hand, he trudged down what seemed like the longest of hallways and back to his room. He opened the closet door, hung the wet towel up on the coat hanger nail and flopped backwards full length on his bed. This day would stand out like several others of late, but for much less wonderful reasons. The Book of O had almost killed him.

CHAPTER SEVENTEEN

Several days passed. Nicholas gradually recovered from his illness. His stomach felt much better after he threw up that first afternoon, but his fever with its aches and pains took longer to go away. The long summer days dragged by while he stayed at home reading Jules Verne's "Journey to the Center of The Earth," watching Andy Griffith reruns on TV, and steering clear of his mother as much as he could.

Sometimes during his brief, but not altogether painless illness, he would sit upstairs on his bed and think. In the middle of the day, he would daydream to his heart's content; let his mind roam free wherever it wanted to take him. Then he would whip it back from China, Timbuktu, Saskatchewan or wherever it had gone and review the events of the past weeks.

He missed the old hollow tree and his favorite spot by the river, both of which had been seriously damaged if not completely destroyed. But now he had the Book of O. It had appeared mysteriously, not unlike the old tree, and given him such an earth shattering push over the edge of his ordinary life.

Tyco had also given Nicholas' world a shake. He and his merry troupe of dwarves had inspired Nicholas so much. They were like Nicholas' family. He could never forget them. One day again, he hoped to meet them all and romp through Oberron.

While he could sometimes tell himself what he was going to dream about before he slept, he hadn't been able to make himself dream about the dwarves. That didn't really bother him too much though. One interesting event would always lead him to another.

Lucy had told him of her dream symbol with the three concentric rings around the perfect triangle (he had later read that perfect triangles were also called isosceles.) Her symbol had given him the beautiful vision of his homeland, an alien planet somewhere in the far flung universe (a weird concept, but he did believe in it.) This alien planet had two suns and a turquoise ocean, at the bottom of which stood a great white city of light with a gold and silver temple.

Even the amber silken creature at the bottom of the crystal pool had given him a treasure, an encouraging message in a language as beautiful and unusual as the land with two suns. He missed all these things, though he knew that none of them were truly gone. His dreams were real, even if they were sometimes symbolic.

Most people didn't think dreams were real or had much value, but he knew things they didn't. He felt sorry for those people. Perhaps that was a form of compassion like the Eastern monks had suggested he learn.

Nicholas did want to help people, but he knew now the best way to do that. He cared about the Earth and as the Earth Champion he would do his best to protect her. Even so he knew he couldn't fight any battle or perform any miracles that didn't begin by making his own heart pure. That was probably why he had gotten sick, to purify himself. The Book of O had much to teach him. It couldn't do that if he were clogged with extra baggage.

The Book of O had become his friend even though it had started an avalanche of trouble that broke loose inside him. Maybe that was part of what friends need to do for each other sometimes. Part of his sickness had to do with his stubbornness. He didn't want to move away from Flat Rock. His familiar haunts and places to go were all here, as well as the people he knew, some of them since he was a small child. These things would be no more, not like before.

Most of all, he would miss Lucy. He'd never felt as close to anyone in his life. Oh well, he'd have to let it all go, even the land with two suns. It would be wonderful to see it again, but he couldn't hold on to such things. His mission was to go on, always go on, and leave behind those people and things he loved. If they met again one day then that would be great but...

The "Book of O" still lay on his nightstand beside the bed. He hadn't touched it since the last time he'd seen Lucy. He reached over and picked up the book, then lay back on his bed with his head on two thick pillows. As if on cue, a pleasant breeze blew in through his window. The curtains fluttered as the elm tree whistled outside. Nicholas felt better just holding the book, squeezing it gently between both hands, edge up. He placed his thumbs squarely in the center of the thick volume and cleared his mind. What would the book say?

At the top of a middle page he saw a bold title.
"THE FIRST OF ALL RIDDLES."
Beneath the title the paragraph began.

> *The businessman pulled on the lapels of his seersucker suit, adjusted the knot of his boldly striped black and gold tie and strode forward. He carried a brief case by its handle in his hand and a look of confidence on his clear features as he squinted into the sun setting behind the city.*
>
> *The man's burgundy briefcase was the same color as his suit, as were his shiny leather shoes and thin belt around his waist. His narrow golden belt buckle and cuff links glistened in the light as he came closer and closer. Everything about the man seemed straightforward and upstanding.*

Hayden, a young lad of twelve with the blackest of hair, complete with a cowlick in front and thick eyebrows, stood in the plaza staring at the man fascinated. Hayden believed the man to be exactly as he presented himself, an honest businessman on his way to some important meeting, no doubt with successful executives somewhere in the city.

As Nicholas read "The Book of O" he found himself becoming very much charged with an incredible energy coursing through his veins. A pinkish gold light emanated from the pages of the book, building in intensity, until it engulfed him in a huge ball of light that filled the room. Even though it was half open, the wind blew with such a powerful force that the glass shattered and scattered on the floor. His room filled with an incredible wind sweeping in through the window. The ball of light spun Nicholas about as the story sucked him in and the wind tore at his clothes. "The Book of O" pulled him into the pages, down into the words, and then pushed him out with a whoosh, into the story.

He landed calmly on his feet in the story plaza. Now, he too could see the tall buildings and the people hurrying about. The businessman in the burgundy suit stood before him in living color. Egads, he was in the story! He had become Hayden!

Somehow it had happened. By the power of the "Book of O," it had happened. Nicholas scrunched up his shoulders, feeling his new body as he looked down at himself. His body was a lot like his old one, young and elastic, but instead of a T-shirt and blue jeans, he wore a red number 29 football jersey. Oh my, oh oh. Yes oh, "The Book of O" had done this. He held out his arms. The fine hairs growing there were no longer golden brown, but black. These were Hayden's arms. They had to be. He had changed, but maybe this would be all right. He felt just fine. What a big city it was, such tall buildings!

Hayden shuddered. It was almost like a cold wind had swept through the plaza, but there was none. He shrugged it off as an oddity. For some reason, "The Book of O" popped in his mind. Where did that bizarre title come from? He shrugged that off too and raised his hand to get the businessman's attention. He certainly would like to talk to the man.

The businessman's face went suddenly out of focus, then his body went out of focus, his clothes too, all suddenly a blur to Hayden. At first Hayden thought he was seeing things, but then he realized the businessman was changing, becoming someone else. The man's clear features became the rough and heavier ones of a completely different man, someone with curly reddish brown hair and fair skin, slightly freckled. Perhaps the new man was Irish. He wore a tweed jacket and woolen pants, carried a long white meerschaum pipe in one hand and smiled winsomely at Hayden.

Hayden hoped the man was a friendly Irishman. As if on command, the man offered his right hand to Hayden with a smile.

"Pappy McGee at your service," he said in a thick Irish accent. Hayden took his hand wholeheartedly.

Hayden realized then that he had created Pappy McGee out of his own need to talk to someone friendly and kind. Maybe the appearance of the businessman had also been the result of his desires. Both the Irishman and the businessman were the same person, but who that was he couldn't be sure. As if sensing Hayden's confusion, the Irishman turned and walked away, quickly disappearing in the crowd of passersby.

The two men, or should he say one, were very interesting. They had sprung from his own imagination, a deeper imagination that he had ever used before. This imagination was so strong it could make Hayden see whatever he wanted to see in people. Hayden's deeper imagination seriously affected how a person appeared and whom he judged them to be, a tricky situation at best. He had to be more careful in the future. Though he had liked both characters, he must let people be themselves and not who he wanted them to be, so he could see them for who they truly were.

Hayden wandered up the street feeling disenchanted. He turned up an alley between two run-down three-story brick buildings. What a strange situation. The two separate men lived in one body. That was unusual and a bit disturbing. Could it be possible that more than one person lived inside his own body?

Man, this place reeked of rotten garbage. He kicked at an empty beer can in the gutter, sending it flying before him. Maybe you lived more than one life and came back in different bodies. Maybe you only lived one long continuous life in many different bodies at different times, but just called them separate lives. There were many possibilities.

At the end of the alleyway, he entered a side street, unpaved and full of mud holes. Boring houses, old and run down, the kind you could see in the poor section of almost any town lined both sides of the street. A rusty old pick-up as dirty as the street came chugging slowly by and stopped at the stop sign. Just as it started taking off, Hayden grabbed the top of the closed tailgate and ducked down, hoping the driver wouldn't notice him. With the toes of his tennis shoes, he perched on the bumper then squatted down as the pick-up gained speed.

It raced ahead much faster than Hayden had expected, lurching one way then the other as if the driver tried to throw him. At one point, the driver actually went clear out of his way to run smack dab in the middle of a huge puddle, splashing the sides of the pick-up as well as Hayden.

As the pick-up slowed down and stopped at the next intersection, Hayden jumped off and marched around to the driver's window, infuriated. His clothes were soaked and his face splattered with gobs of mud.

"Listen you wise guy," he said between clenched teeth as he approached the window. The driver wore a greasy hooded sweatshirt, but when he turned his head, Hayden got a full view of his face. He had a scruffy salt and pepper beard, pockmarked skin, and two deep grooves running from his forehead down to the bridge of his large bulb of a nose. His small menacing brown eyes seemed to laugh at Hayden.

"What you want, you lousy bum?" the man spurted. "Thought you could get a free ride, eh?"

Hayden slowly grabbed the pick-up door handle and pushed the button in with his thumb.

"Nobody gets a free ride from Dominus," the man continued. I've..."

Hayden whipped open the door and grabbed the man by his sweatshirt and hauled him out from his seat. With superhuman strength, Nicholas held the man up with one hand and with the other punched him beneath the rib cage, piercing the man's flesh with the knuckles of his fist, ramming them upward. He squeezed Dominus by one of his soft puffy lungs and yelled directly into his face, "Do you know who I am? I could kill you as easy as this."

Surprised at himself and his poisonous anger, Hayden let go of Dominus' lung. Dominus wheezed as Hayden pulled his arm out from beneath Dominus' chest, making a wet suction sound with a pop at the end. As if nothing had happened, the wound closed neatly, no trace of blood. Dominus fell back in his seat, dumbstruck, a look of horror on his face.

Hayden felt disgusted with himself as he walked away from the truck. Scaring Dominus had given him no pleasure whatsoever. It had made him sick with his own inflated self-importance. What a horrible thing to do. No doubt the guy was a jerk, but what did that make Hayden, some kind of monster? Hayden hadn't known such outrageous anger lurked inside him. How could it spring out so easily like that? He didn't like it one bit.

He made his way back to the heart of the city and downtown, not knowing what else to do or where to go. He found himself standing just a short while later in front of a tall skyscraper, before a tall glass and brass revolving door.

Hayden was surprised to see his sixteen-year-old brother Arthur, leaning against the building as if waiting for a photo opportunity, one ankle crossed over the other, inspecting his nails. He had his slick thick black hair combed back off his forehead and dark Clark Kent type glasses, which he took off and stuffed in his shirt pocket when he saw Hayden. Everyone thought Arthur was cool, except Hayden. Hayden just liked him.

"Hey, Hayden," his brother said and grinned.

Arthur always said, hey Hayden. Hayden didn't mind. It made him feel kind of special. "Can I buy you a drink at the bar?" Arthur said as he unzipped his smart yellow cotton jacket. He had it off and slung over his shoulder before Hayden could reply.

Hayden pinched his nose with his thumb and forefinger. In a comical nasal tone, he said, "Hey, Art, did you let a fart?" It was his standard comeback. They had performed this little ritual a thousand and one times.

Hayden knew there was no bar inside the building, at least he didn't think so, but he did want to see the place. He stepped into the revolving doors and pushed. They silently glided around the center pole and within seconds he was inside. Arthur came through the doors behind Hayden and pushed him as he entered the hall. Hayden tried to push Arthur back, but his brother jumped ahead and walked off as if he owned the place.

Huge sparkling crystal chandeliers illuminated the hallway, from the bronze columns to the farthest reaches of the vaulted ceilings. People hurried about, going here and there, upstairs, in and out of elevators, across the marble floors, every which way.

As they entered an even larger hall, Arthur brought out a wadded up piece of paper from his jean jacket and handed it to Hayden. Hayden unfolded the paper and glanced at it, then took a second look to make sure he had read the bold typeface correctly. *The Second Door*, hmm, those words seemed familiar, but he couldn't place them. He really had no idea what they meant.

"What's this for?" he asked as he offered the paper to his brother.

"For a while," Arthur replied, refusing the paper. "I've got a thousand just like that one at home in a safe."

Sometimes Hayden just couldn't get a straight answer from his brother. He stuffed it in his pocket feeling uncertain. That would have to do for now. They had just come in one door, but so far no second.

Suddenly he realized that almost all the people of the building had gone out through the revolving door. A few stragglers trotted past, as if fleeing for their lives, going in the same direction the two brothers had just come from. The business day must be at a close. Something was up.

A glass and wooden case built into the smooth granite wall caught Hayden's attention. Arthur and he walked toward it. The closer they got, the more Hayden's interest grew. Two great broad swords, brilliant and magnificent with long silver blades and finely wrought handles of gold, lay in the case on two separate shelves. Man, those must have cost a penny or two!

"Look at this writing Hayden," Arthur said.

Beneath the case was a bronze plaque with two words printed at the top.

Who's Who

Beneath this curious title was a long list of names in three columns bordered by the strangest pagan looking symbols. In the border, Hayden recognized a pentagram and the symbols for the planets Venus and Mercury. There were many others that he didn't recognize.

"Hayden," Arthur said, pointing to the middle of the second column on the bronze plaque. Arthur's jaw hung loose in awe. "Our names!"

Hayden felt a powerful jolt of energy travel from his belly all the way down to his feet. Arthur was right. Both his brother's and his name were bronzed on the plaque, Arthur Finkle and beneath it Hayden Finkle.

"This must be ancient, " Arthur said. "How did we get on this Who's Who thing anyway?"

"I don't know," Hayden replied," but it does look old. It must be some record of some kind."

"Duh, Huck," Arthur said. "You could have fooled me."

Arthur always called him Huck for short and sometimes Huck Fin when he was feeling in a particularly good mood. Arthur said Huck Fin was short for Hayden Finkle. Their names on the list had stirred something deep in Hayden's memory. He had either done great things in his past or he would again. It all depended on...

"Hayden, look." Arthur now pointed at the sword on the top shelf of the case.

Hayden pressed his face up to the glass as Arthur did, trying to see what the fuss was about.

"See those tiny initials on the handle of that sword?" Arthur said.

Two silver initials, an H and an F, ever so small were emblazoned on the sword handle. What a coincidence. The initials were the same as Hayden's.

Looking down at the bottom sword, Hayden smiled and said, "A.F. That bottom sword has the initials A.F. on it. Arthur Kafinkle."

"Do you suppose they're for us?" Arthur asked, ignoring the additional syllable on their last name.

"They must be," Hayden replied as he grabbed the two wooden knobs in the middle of the case and opened the doors. Arthur tucked the top of his jacket inside the waist of his jeans to free his hands, then reached in and took out the bottom sword by the handle, the heavy blade trailing behind on the glass with a screech.

Hayden's hands moved as if on their own, wrapping his fingers around the smooth sword handle and with a determined tug, plucked it from the shelf.

The sword, though heavy, felt lighter than he had expected. He moved it from side to side, blade pointing straight up catching the light. What would he do with such a thing? He glanced at Arthur who just stood, holding his sword, both hands in front of him; point downward, smiling at Hayden. That was too strange. For a second, he had seen Arthur wearing a shining suit of silver armor, complete with helmet and visor. No, he couldn't have. Oh well, such is life. It only got stranger by the minute.

"Ladies and gentleman, Hayden shouted out, "I give you the honorable King Arthur."

A side door clicked shut. Hayden turned to see Dominus standing before it. Oh no, not him again. Dominus wore a clean gray cloak, hood down, showing off masses of dread locks that stuck out in clumps at all angles. He held a long broad sword in one hand, poised with knees bent as if he were ready to attack.

Hayden cringed. If only he hadn't pounded Dominus so before. He didn't feel superhuman anymore at all. Something had killed his powers.

Hayden knew Arthur and he were in for it the second he heard another side door shut with a loud click. An even bigger man stood beside Dominus wearing a long black robe. He had a mean leathery face with black eyes that looked greedily from Hayden to Arthur. He snarled at the brothers then and reached inside his robe. With a sliding metallic ka-ching that echoed throughout the hall, he drew out a long broadsword from a scabbard at his side. He raised the sword high.

"Ho there Borius," Dominus said. "These two would be mincemeat before the day is done."

Hayden knew that neither Arthur nor he had the slightest idea how to fight with swords. Even so he found himself circling about to his right, one foot crossing over the other as he stepped as softly as a wary cat. Arthur stepped lightly beside him, imitating his brother.

"What do you do here, little ones?" Borius grunted. "Want to play?"

All four sword carriers circled about, Hayden and Arthur on one side and Borius and Dominus on the other. Then with a great metallic clash of a gong that rang out from above, Borius and Dominus charged, crossing the floor much more quickly than expected, slashing down at the youngsters with their swords. Hayden raised his own sword sideways over his head to block Dominus's blow. The two swords clashed together with a jarring impact that nearly broke Hayden's arm. He took several steps backward to gain time. He didn't want this, didn't want this at all.

Hayden glanced at Arthur to see him blocking one of Borius' sword strokes. The resonant sound made his teeth hurt. Arthur retreated with Hayden, staying as close to him as he possibly could.

"We have to get out of here," Arthur croaked hoarsely.

Hayden felt horribly out of place and out of time. Then his sword disappeared, right out from under his very nose. Now what would he do? He looked to Arthur still stepping backwards. His sword too was gone.

Hayden grabbed Arthur by the collar of his T-shirt and pulled him backwards with him. Without a word, they both turned and ran, back to the farthest reaches of the hall, looking for a way out.

Borius and Dominus laughed as one, their uproarious chuckles spelling doom for the youngsters. They stood before the exit, solid and tall with feet spread apart like two crazed buffaloes.

No door could the two brothers find and no window could they open, not a way out anywhere could they see. Dominus wasted no time taking advantage of their predicament. His sword started stretching out upwards as if it were made of elastic rubber. Dominus' silver blade grew longer and longer, forming a huge arc that spanned the distance between the exit and the two youngsters. It easily searched for them like a heat-seeking missile, the deadly point of the blade only a few feet away now, arcing down at them.

Hayden didn't give in to fear though the sword blade threatened. Somehow he felt that if he didn't the sword couldn't harm them. Even so he had to quickly come up with a plan.

Three small children, a girl and two boys sat on a rug in the corner beneath the stairs. They played a board game and chewed something that made their cheeks bulge. Like animals eating their kill, afraid that others would steal it, the children looked suspiciously at the two intruders. These kids must be related to Dominus.

Hayden took another look at Dominus' approaching sword point. The dark-haired one of the two little girls swallowed her candy with a gulp and stared bug eyed at Hayden. A spark of kindness showed in her eyes, not a full-fledged thing, but enough. Hayden raised his hand toward Arthur to still him and closed his eyes, focused on that caring part that he felt in the little girl.

Hayden had a flash then that the key to the Second Door was inside his mind. The Second Door was their way out. His forehead throbbed with intense energy. Inside his head, he saw bright lights, shocking purple and blue, which turned to green, then turquoise, his favorite. The turquoise swirled about and flowed into a circle of light that spun and spiraled inward and downward like a beautiful tornado.

Hayden opened his eyes. The turquoise spiral had become a long narrow tube that expanded as he waited. Then knowing that Dominus' sword point would soon be upon them and trusting that this was the way to escape, he jumped feet forward into the tube. Ah, the pure ecstasy of relief as he fell, free fall, downward. He had found the Second Door. Looking up he could see Arthur falling down through the tunnel above him. They had made it. They would be all right now. They had found the Second Door.

The colorful tube turned gradually and the brothers slid side by side on their bottoms down the slick surface. Eventually they slowed and stopped altogether, their legs hanging out in front of them at the opening to a room.

A small boy with shaven head, wearing a silk robe of gold and green and two grown men in similar robes, their heads also shaven, stood around a small circular wooden stand about three feet high. The room was dimly lit, but as the little boy reached into his robe and brought out the whitest of white balls, the whole room radiated with a white light. Hayden could barely see the two men and the boy now, just the white ball of light. The little boy had apparently placed it on the center of the stand where it spun freely about as if liquid glass.

Automatically, as if it had a will of its own, Hayden's left arm rose, and then bent at the elbow. The tip of his ring finger and thumb touched lightly, forming a circle. His remaining fingers extended upward and Hayden's mind became lost in an indescribable happiness. The little boy sang a song, a vibrant melody that lifted them all as time stood still.

CHAPTER EIGHTEEN

Nicholas didn't move and barely inhaled a long slow breath that seemed to go on and on. He felt on the outside of time. A powerful chant vibrated throughout his body and mind, the strange words in a foreign language that tugged at his soul. Then he realized that he was singing the chant and it stopped. He opened his eyes. He was sitting up in bed, his heart beating slowly, his legs straight out, his left arm raised, elbow bent. His fingers on that hand curled slightly, except for the first one, which pointed straight up. Electricity surged up through his body and out his fingertips. He could feel the energy everywhere, in his body, in the bed beneath him, the room itself and most of all the air that he breathed. He allowed the incredible pleasant force to hold him in place, a position so comfortable and unusual that he hesitated to move.

The "Book of O" lay open in his lap. That had been it then! Yes, now he remembered. The book had started his adventure as Hayden, but had he been asleep or awake? Had it all been a dream? He couldn't be sure. Maybe it didn't really matter.

His right hand tingled. He lowered his left hand and looked at his right, dumbfounded. The soft fleshy part beneath his thumb was bruised a muddy shade of mottled purple and yellow. Whoa, that was where he had felt the blow of Dominus' mighty sword. Too cool. His hand didn't hurt much though, just a slight ache that faded. It boggled him how the bruise could carry over from his book adventure.

He must have slept through from yesterday afternoon all the way into this morning. So much had happened in his trip or dream or whatever it was. He could hardly remember it all, but he did remember being wide-awake when he had opened the book and the adventure began.

First had been the businessman and the Irishman. Nicholas had to be more careful how he looked at people in the future. It was so easy to be fooled. That must be part of the First of All Riddles, how to see people for who they truly were, instead of who you want them to be. Just because it sounded corny, doesn't mean that it is corny.

His brother Arthur, a character Nicholas had never dreamed existed had appeared. The list of Who's Who with the beautiful swords along with Dominus and Laborious had added so much to his experience, some of which he could have lived without. The children and the Second Door were not in that group for sure.

The final episode featured the little boy with the white ball and his two monk friends. They had given Nicholas such courage. The whole string of events had made him feel that he could accomplish anything. It just wouldn't do to get stuck in fear. If you did, you could just go round and round like that revolving door Arthur and Hayden had gone through. It must have been the first door. The Second Door must be the opening to the turquoise tunnel that he found in his mind.

Nicholas felt refreshed from his adventure with "The Book of O". As he got out of bed and busied himself taking a shower, he remembered they were moving to Colorado today. That gave him a curious feeling, one he'd never had. Just how would the move turn out?

The moving van was probably outside already. He looked out his bedroom window as he buttoned his shirt. The yellow and black moving van was parked in front of their house by the curb. A long ramp ran from its back end to the paved street. His parent's car sat off to the right in the driveway, an old, but refinished blue gray Ventura Pontiac in excellent shape.

A big fellow in a brown jump suit and a black lower back support wrapped around his waist slammed his door and jumped down from the running board of the van to the curb, clipboard in hand. This moving thing was becoming too real.

Nicholas looked across the street. All he could see of Lucy's house were a few brown patches of stucco between the dancing branches of the elm trees. How long had it been since he had seen her?

Strange that she hadn't come to see him once since he'd been sick. She must have thought that he needed the time alone for a while. He wished he could have some of that time back now. Lucy and he would barely have a chance to say goodbye.

"Nicholas," his mother yelled from the bottom of the stairs. "We have to get packed up now."

Her words shocked him, though he knew they would have to go soon. Nicholas's mother had been quite busy boxing everything up getting ready to go while he was sick. Everything seemed crystal clear now. The "Book of O" had made him sick, but it had also cleared out his head and his heart. He really didn't dread moving all that much now. In fact he looked forward to the adventure waiting in Colorado and the Rocky Mountains, but...

"Nicholas, are you coming down or not?" his mother yelled.

"I'm coming," he yelled back.

He sat on the bed to collect himself. His mother was so pushy sometimes. Things were moving too fast. The "Book of O" was all he really wanted to pack. Well, there were a few other things, but they weren't nearly as important. The book was a treasure unlike any other. The bookseller had no idea what he had sold Lucy that Saturday morning.

He looked over at the book lying on his nightstand. The big silver O on the cover might not be an o at all, but some other symbol, maybe a scientific or spiritual one. He really had no idea. The book could come from somewhere really far away, somewhere not even on Earth. The way the cup shaped flowers grew on the stalks of grain made the plant look unlike any he'd ever seen. He felt drawn to the book even now as they were preparing to leave. Maybe the book was from another planet, like the one with two red suns. Jumping Jehosophat, the book could read his mind and take him incredible places to teach him! What more could he ask for? He longed to open the book to see what it would say or do.

The low thud of furniture banging about down below brought him to his senses. It wouldn't do to upset his parents, not today of all days. He got up from the bed and hurried downstairs.

His parents both stood in the living room with their hands on their hips, watching the movers carry out the sofa. Nicholas couldn't figure out his dad. His dad never let anyone lift anything really heavy unless he was in on it himself.

His dad's engineer overalls fit tight and without his shirt on you could plainly see the muscles of his upper body. He must be as strong as Hercules. Well, maybe not quite that strong, but the years of lifting, pushing, and carrying plaster and planks had made him much more than just fit. Some of his father's workers had told Nicholas how his father always won his arm wrestling contests at the bars. Though his father never mentioned the arm wrestling, Nicholas believed the workers' story.

His mother covered her mouth with her hand, horrified. The tall skinny mover had just missed hitting the corner of their shiny walnut coffee table as he carried it out the front door.

"Come on Nicholas," she said; "let's you and me finish packing up your room. It's the only one we haven't done yet."

"There are a few things in the basement we need to box," his father said, pounding one end of his Camel cigarette against the flat of his palm. He always tamped the tobacco that way so the loose leaves wouldn't fall out. He put the cigarette in his mouth, got out his Zippo lighter from his hip pocket, flipped it open and struck the flint igniter with his thumb. As the cigarette blazed, he took a big drag. A look of supreme pleasure came over his face.

His mother with eyes wide watched the shorter moving guy carry two heavy looking glass lamps, one in each hand, out the front door. "Oh, all right," his mother finally responded. "You go up to your room, Nicholas. I'll be up in a minute."

Nicholas climbed the stairs, feeling like a yo-yo. First, she wanted him to come down, now go up, and then down again. He didn't feel terribly strong yet, but the excitement of the move had started to infect him.

In his room, he broke down his computer and got out its box from the top shelf of his closet. It wouldn't take long to pack. He really didn't have that much. Within minutes he had the computer monitor, the printer, the keyboard and all the cables fit snugly inside their Styrofoam molds in their special boxes.

His erector set city on his desk took only seconds to dismantle. He enjoyed destroying the skyscraper buildings as if he had the power of Godzilla or King Kong. Then he remembered he had to call his Uncle Caleb.

He raced down the stairs to the kitchen and dialed his uncle's number on their rotary phone mounted on the wall. Looking up at the Garfield comic strip cartoon taped on the wall above the phone, he listened to the number ring. Sometimes his uncle took his own sweet time. Maybe the fish had all died. He hoped not.

"Hello," a husky voice finally answered.

"Uncle Caleb?"

"Yes?"

"This is Nicholas."

"Uh huh."

"I hope you know I've been sick most of the week. That's why I didn't get out to see the fish."

"No, I didn't know. Sorry to hear that."

"That's okay. I'm better now." He hesitated, afraid to ask about the fish. If they all had died, he just couldn't stand it.

"Do you think those fish will be all right?"

"Well... His uncle dragged out the word well, changing its pitch three different times as if it actually had three syllables. "I don't know."

"What do you mean?" Nicholas asked, peeling the corner of the Garfield cartoon from the wall. "Didn't they live?"

"Oh, yeah, well, they'll mostly live, but..."

The comic strip tore in half as he tugged upon it.

"I don't know what I'm going to do with them," his uncle continued.

"What do you mean?"

"Why, there's so many of 'em."

"Yeah, but you said you had room for them in your pond."

"I did."

"What do you mean you did?" Nicholas had reached his limit.

"They must have had an awful lot of little ones 'cuz now there's more'n three times as many."

"Really?"

"Yep, but don't you worry none. Phineas Wake said he's got a pond over his way where we can stock 'em if we want."

"Cool, thanks."

"Then there's always the creek too if we get an extra overflow," his uncle added. "Don't you worry none."

Nicholas' felt relieved. His uncle was so cool.

"You folks gettin' ready to take off today?"

"Yeah," Nicholas replied on a somewhat down note, "but we'll be back soon I think... to visit."

"Sure, you will. Sure, you will. I'm coming into town here pretty soon. Maybe I can catch ya before ya go."

"Okay, it won't be long. See you when you get here."

After he hung up, Nicholas felt like a chapter in his life had closed. The fish meant so much to him. All those times he'd spent at the river had been great, skipping stones, catching frogs and snakes, just looking around even, dreaming his life away by himself, sometimes with a friend. If the fish lived it would be easier for his dreams to live. They would have a place to go.

He peeled the rest of the comic strip from the wall. It was the last thing to go from the kitchen. There was nothing left here but a yellow room and a bunch of bare white cupboards.

Walking toward the living room, he paused at the doorway, his body hidden behind the kitchen wall, his head peeking around the corner. His mom and dad stood inside the outline on the carpet where the sofa had once sat. His dad lit a cigarette. His mom looked at her pocket size notebook, pencil in hand. Both movers must be outdoors. The living room looked pretty bare, just a couple of small boxes at his parents feet.

For a moment, he watched his parents in silence, two people striking out in a new direction, taking a chance. Nicholas imagined that he was in his mother's body, recalling the feeling he had awakened with that morning. Time stood still again.

He could feel the threads of time and space wrapped around his mother like a web. She struggled against time, fearing that there was never enough of it. Her calculations made her panic as she checked her list. There wouldn't be enough room to fit everything in the truck. It would be just as hard to find a space for her in the future. Life was a competition. You have to make space for yourself. Competition was all that she knew, but she would struggle on.

Nicholas switched from his mother to his father, imagining that he puffed on the Camel cigarette. The tobacco smoke filled his lungs, easing his doubts. How could he afford all of this? There was never enough, yet he hoped things would work out. One never knows.

The two hired moving men came in the front door and looked around the bare room.

"Upstairs then," his father pointed with a flip of the wrist. "I'll give you a hand."

Nicholas stepped through the doorway, passing the three men walking toward the kitchen. His mother looked as if she were going to cry, though she never did, not that he'd ever seen. He stepped over to her and started rolling up the short sleeve of her white cotton blouse. She didn't seem to notice at first. He continued to roll up her sleeve, exposing her tan line and the pale skin of her upper arm, but finally she realized what he was doing and gave him a swat on the shoulder.

"Stop that!" she scolded, chuckling in spite of herself as she slapped him on the hand. Nicholas rolled her sleeve back down. She knew that he understood her, but she would never say a thing. You didn't talk about your feelings much in his family.

"Suppose you'll miss this place?" he asked, bending down to look in one of the boxes.

"Oh, I don't know, some."

Nicholas squatted on the floor with his back to his mother. He could imagine her with her right arm across her chest, her hand supporting her left elbow, her left hand upon her chin, little finger curled to her lips in her favorite concentration pose.

"Have you packed everything in the attic already?" he asked, pulling one flap of the box open.

"Uh huh. Your room is the last."

The short stocky mover walked out with one of Nicholas' computer boxes. Nicholas looked over his shoulder at her and smiled. She had struck the very pose he had imagined she would, standing there gazing out the window as if she were lost. Frozen, that's what she was. She didn't want to feel anything.

On the top of the stack inside the box he was looking in, he found the psychology magazine on dreams his mother and he had read from together. Beneath it was the picture of his brother Ethan from her attic trunk.

"What are these doing in here?" he asked.

"I thought you might like to have them out in your new room when we get to Colorado."

He turned again to look at her. She looked very sad. Nicholas felt sorry for her. She just couldn't deal with the past. Her life must seem such a loss to her.

His father and the tall mover came through the living room, lugging Nicholas' desk. His mother grabbed a box beside him. "Let's take these out," she said, marching for the door.

There was nothing Nicholas could do for her. She might want to stay locked up inside herself for a long time. She had that disease where she was stuck in the past without knowing it, avoiding all the horrible experiences that once were, surrounded by them but untouched.

He picked up the box and looked around the living room. It looked barren, not a thing left, except the blue carpet and the curtains, two dingy old things that had once been white, framing the picture window. There had been some good times here, to be sure, but he had a feeling that the future would be a lot better.

Man! He had almost forgotten his book. He raced up the stairs with the box under his arm and flung open his bedroom door. The book still lay on his nightstand. Had anyone touched it or opened it? It looked undisturbed. He took it in his free hand and stepped to the window.

Down in the yard, Lucy stood on the grass, talking with his mother. Lucy looked as beautiful as could be. His father and the hired movers were coming up the walk. What would he say to Lucy? He suddenly felt so bad for her and for himself.

When he got downstairs and out to the yard, his Uncle Caleb had arrived in his beat up old International pick-up. The green bomb was parked in front of the van at the curb. His uncle stood by his mother, talking to Lucy as if they were old friends. His hands moved before him, signing his words as if he were an Indian scout. His crème-colored cowboy hat was pushed back from his forehead. It was a very hot day. His uncle seemed to have an attentive audience in Lucy and his mother.

"Hey, Nick," his uncle said as Nicholas walked across the lawn toward them. Lucy turned and gave Nicholas an open look that shook him. How could she be so calm? Maybe being fourteen had its benefits.

"I got somethin' for ya," his uncle said.

"Just a minute," he said. "I'll put this box in the truck." He avoided everyone's eyes. Now he didn't want to show his feelings.

On his way to the truck, he imagined telling everyone exactly how he felt about him or her, right in front of each other on the lawn. He could tell them how he felt about so many things, his love for Lucy, his fear of losing her, his gratefulness toward his uncle, even his impossible wish to help his mother. He would show them all of these feelings and more by actually spilling his guts. They would plop out in a pile on the grass, a steaming mass of curling intestines. That would surprise them.

His fantasy gave him a boost. He chuckled to himself out loud as he tossed the box in the back of the truck. Why did he have to take things so seriously? What he would really like to do, that is if he was really brave and there were enough time, would be to take each one of these people aside in private and talk to them. That too was impossible. He knew his fantasy was strange, but harmless.

As he walked back over to the small group of three gathered on the lawn, the fantasy didn't go away. He imagined his guts still lying on the grass in the center of the group. He didn't really wish for the fantasy to stay, but stay it did. To make matters goofier, he imagined giving his pile of intestines on the grass a kick with his foot. They didn't disappear. It was fine with him if his guts wanted to stay on the lawn. Did other people have such crazy fantasies?

Lucy and his mother watched his uncle, who with one hand made wavy lines in the air as if drawing a sign for water. Nicholas caught the word "pond" in the middle of his uncle's sentence. That got Nicholas' attention. "To fill three tubs with fish," his uncle said, and then added, "Hey, Nick, ole boy." His uncle put down his hands and looked sideways at Nicholas. "I'll bet you're just plain tuckered out."

Nicholas felt confused. His uncle always caught him off guard, one of the points he liked about him.

"Well, aren't you?" his uncle asked.

Lucy grinned. His mother looked curious.

"What do you mean?" Nicholas asked, smiling. Whenever he asked that question, his uncle usually had something funny to say.

"After moving all that furniture," his uncle said, smiling wide, showing a mouth full of gleaming white teeth.

"Oh, yeah, "Nicholas said with his thumbs in his back pockets. He sucked in a big breath through his mouth, puffed up his chest and like a macho man said, "Me and the boys are just about done."

His mother chuckled and swatted him with the back of her hand. Nicholas let go of his breath with a gush of air and cackled with laughter like an old man. He could always count on Uncle Caleb.

A silence came over the group then as each one looked at the others. As quick as a gunslinger on the draw, his uncle stuffed both of his hands into the front pockets of his Wranglers, and then whipped them back out again curled up in fists that he held straight out palms down before Nicholas.

Lucy and his mom both looked clueless. Nicholas had played this game before. Sometimes he chose the hand with something in it and sometimes he didn't, but he always felt that he won because his uncle would always give him something really cool.

Nicholas still had the gifts that his uncle had given him over the years. He remembered a blackened petrified dinosaur tooth from a T-rex dug up out at the bottom of one of the sand pits outside of town, a brand new jackknife with a shiny mother-of-pearl handle, a small harmonica that Nicholas still loved to play, and other great gifts that he had stashed in a shoebox somewhere. The shoebox would be going with them on the move. He'd find it when they got to Colorado.

One of his favorite presents to get from his uncle was a jawbreaker, hard round candies shaped like a very small ball that you could suck on forever. Yes, he liked them the best, because that always meant his uncle would spend quite a lot of time with Nicholas. His uncle would play the guess what's in which hand game. When Nicholas chose, he'd always get the right hand then, because both his uncle's hands had jawbreakers in them, one for Nicholas and one for his uncle. His uncle and he would pop them in their mouths and laugh at each other, because they both looked like squirrels with nuts bulging in their mouths. Then they would spend the day fishing or driving around his uncle's farm. They would see prairie dogs in their prairie dog towns or maybe find a turtle crossing the road in the middle of a hot day.

It had been quite a while since his uncle had played the guess-which-hand-it's-in game, but Nicholas knew there wouldn't be a jawbreaker in his uncle's hand today. They had to leave too soon for that.

His uncle's hands looked old and weather cracked, but his face shone brightly like a child's with mischief, his dark brown eyes full of joy. Nicholas tapped his uncle's right hand on the knuckles with his finger. His uncle's hand flipped open, revealing a rough but beautiful blue stone lying in his palm. The clear deep turquoise color of the stone took Nicholas' breath away. He stared at it, speechless.

The blue stone looked just like the dream one Lenora had given him when they shared memories in Oberron.

"It's a turquoise," his uncle said, looking from the stone to Nicholas father walking by on the sidewalk. His father carried a pile of long wooden slats from Nicholas' bed. The tallest mover, walking behind his dad, carried Nicholas bed springs and the shorter mover carried his mattress.

Nicholas took the stone from his uncle's hand and held it up in his own, admiring the natural shape and the way dark traces of copper and green set off the sky blue turquoise.

"Need some help there, William?" his uncle yelled.

"No," his father answered, walking past. "We just about have it."

"Now, there's a story that goes with that," his uncle said, pointing to the stone. His uncle popped open a snap on the top of his shirt pocket and brought out a package of Red Man chewing tobacco.

Lucy reached out to touch the stone and cooed, "It's beautiful!" Her hand brushed Nicholas' with loving warmth that soothed him. Lucy's presence felt different today or maybe he had changed. He could feel her more easily than ever.

Tyco had said that dreams and memories were the money of Oberron. Did that mean it wouldn't work in Emkhoura, the name he had given to Earth?

Nicholas' uncle stuffed a wad of tobacco into his mouth and cleared his throat as he began to chew. The tobacco smelled pleasant, a fruity and spicy aroma that always tickled Nicholas nose. He automatically gave it an itch with his finger. The spirit of Lucy's Great Grandfather Ruben had also made Nicholas' nose itch. Without Abraxas and Ruben, he would never have found "The Book of O" that he carried beneath his arm.

"I had a visitor the other day," his uncle finally began in a high pitched whine of a voice that always promised something unusual.

Nicholas' mother crossed her arms as if to ward off evil spirits or keep everything and everyone at a distance. The very fact that she did that so often showed her great sensitivity. She was psychic in her own way, but feared her gift for some reason.

Nicholas felt his mother's intentions as easily as he did Lucy's and his uncle's. Looking at them all was like reading books. His uncle chewed his tobacco, trying to get it situated just so in his mouth so he could continue his story. He looked like the happiest of cows, chewing its cud and preparing his audience for one of his wild tales.

"Now this man's name is Bus Schplitzkrieg," his uncle said with a smile. "I don't know if any of you know him or not, but..." He gave everyone a questioning look. No one responded.

The sound of footsteps coming up the walk distracted Nicholas' uncle. Nicholas' father and the two movers behind him were coming from the truck back up toward the house, all empty handed. His uncle looked torn between his brother William and his attentive little group of listeners.

"Hey, Bill," his uncle said, "you remember ole Bus Schplitzkrieg don't cha?"

"Of course," his father replied, stopping on the walk. The hired movers walked around his father on the grass. His father pulled the shoulder straps of his overalls away from his bare sweating chest. Beads of sweat rolled from his forehead down onto the bridge of his nose. He swallowed once as if that would help him catch his breath.

"He's that big old German fella that lives in that shack over by the creek at the edge of town," his father said. "Why?"

Nicholas sensed tension between his father and his uncle. Some secret thing had happened between the two brothers that he didn't know much about, except that his father rarely spoke to his uncle because of it.

"Oh, I'm just telling these folks a story about him," his uncle said satisfied with himself.

"You would be telling a story," his father said angrily. "That's about all you're good at." He let go of his overall straps, which snapped, against his chest.

Nicholas' uncle brushed his brother away with a gesture of his hand as if he were a king dismissing one of his lowly subjects.

His father looked peeved, about to explode. He held his breath and pursed his lips, then with fists clenched, stamped off toward the house.

Nicholas would like to know what terrible thing had come between his father and his uncle. Another part of him wished they could all just be friends. He felt uncomfortable standing there and a little guilty too, though his mom had already told him that since he had been sick, he didn't have to help them move.

"So anyway," his uncle continued, "to make a long story shorter..." His uncle held his hands out in front of himself to recapture his audience.

"Bus asked me if he could catch some of those carp out of my pond. I told him sure, go ahead, but they're not very good for eating. There are too many bones. Bus said that they were good eatin' if you pressure-cooked 'em up 'till all the bones became so tender you could just eat the whole fish, bones an all. So I let him. I hope you don't mind, Nicholas? You and Lucy went through a lot of trouble for those fish."

"Nah," Nicholas said. "We don't mind, not if someone can make good use of them like that."

"I figured you'd feel that way," his uncle said. "I'm glad. A couple days or so later, Bus drove his rickety old yellow Oldsmobile out to my house just a little excited. He told me that he found that blue stone inside a carp's gullet when he was cleaning the fish."

Lucy and Nicholas shared a look of surprise. Nicholas felt charged. Tyco or Lenora could be watching somehow. The little people had shown up first when Nicholas was dreaming at the river and now this. The stone had appeared just like it had in his dream. That made the Little People all the more real. They were sending him a message through the fish. They hadn't forgotten him.

The stone felt warm in his hands as the late morning sun beat down upon them. Nicholas had never heard of anyone finding a turquoise in Kansas, not in a natural state, but here it was.

"So it's yours," his uncle added, "Yours and Lucy's. Most people would never return such a valuable looking stone as that, but ole Bus is a likeable sort."

It was a gift unlike any other. Nicholas handed the stone to Lucy.

"It's so beautiful," she said, holding it in her palm and stroking it with her slender thumb.

"You keep it," Nicholas said.

Lucy's eyes widened. "Oh Nicholas!"

Nicholas' mother put her hand on Nicholas' shoulder. "I better help your father," she said.

"I'm gonna hit the road, folks," his uncle said, giving Lucy a pat on the back. "You come see me and those fish anytime you want, young lady."

"Goodbye, Caleb," his mother said.

His uncle tipped his cowboy hat as Nicholas' mother walked off.

"Bye, Mrs. O'Malley," Lucy shouted.

Nicholas' mother turned about and waved, walking backwards for a few steps, then turned again and climbed the front steps.

Nicholas' uncle offered him his hand. "You come and see me one of these days Nicholas." Nicholas shifted his book to his left arm and shook his uncle's hand. It might be a long time before he saw his uncle again.

Lucy and Nicholas walked with his uncle over to his pick-up. His uncle got in the truck and stuffed his long thin legs down under the dash to the floorboard. He shut the door, started the truck with a roar of the engine, nodded his head once, and took off.

Nicholas felt that a bright spot in his life had faded. Between his parents grudge against his uncle and his family's move, there was little chance that he would see his uncle for a long time.

Lucy and he watched the pick-up for the longest time as it slowly crept up the long street. It grew smaller and finally turned near the edge of the town where it disappeared altogether.

Nicholas sighed. "Guess we'll have to…" He couldn't finish his sentence. He didn't even know what he was going to say. His mind had gone blank.

Lucy took Nicholas' hand and pulled him down to sit beside her on the curb in front of the van, hidden from his parents view.

"Have you read much in your book?" she asked.

Nicholas hugged the book against his chest. "Some. I'll have to write you and tell you what happened. You wouldn't believe…" He looked at her again. Of course she would believe. She was about the only one that would. He felt too sad and afraid to speak.

The front door of his house slammed shut. The movers must be done. They had already put the screen door back on its hinges. Nicholas bit his upper lip and took a big breath, then let it out with a sigh. Lucy put her hand upon his knee. He felt trapped by his emotions. Now that the big moment had come, he didn't want it. He wanted the pressure to go away. He felt numb. This must be how his mother felt a lot.

He heard his father's deep muffled voice at the other end of the truck, then the heavy van door coming down on its rollers and slamming shut with a bang that he could feel vibrate the concrete curb. His parents would be looking for him.

"Just a sec," he said. "I'll be right back." His parents had mentioned getting gas in their car before they left for Colorado.

Nicholas got up and walked around to the back of the truck. His mother stood beside the tall moving guy, staring at the truck as if she couldn't believe they were actually moving. His father must be around front now talking to the other mover, making arrangements.

"We'll probably be there by dark," the tall mover said. His hair looked greasy, as did his dark blue coveralls. He'd probably done this kind of move a million times. His mother nodded to the man as Nicholas approached her.

"Hey, mom," he said. "Could you and Dad go to the gas station without me? There's something Lucy wants to show me before we leave. Could you come back and pick me up then?"

"Well, all right, but it won't take long. You meet us right here in a few minutes, okay?"

"Sure," he said, feeling better. Now he would have a chance to talk to Lucy.

Lucy stood beside the curb on the grass near the front of the trunk when he returned. She held her hands, clasped inside out in front of her, palms downward. A gentle breeze blew her long loose hair about her face. She looked concerned and curious.

"My parents will come back in a minute to get me. They're going to gas up."

Lucy looked across the street to her house and reached into the pocket of her navy blue skirt. She brought out the turquoise and held it in her palm.

"You know, Lenora traded memories with you in Oberron," Lucy said. "I know. I saw this turquoise when she gave that memory to you. I saw it in my mind as plain as day. And I saw the three rings around the triangle and the land with two suns when you shared your memories with her."

Nicholas was surprised. "I guess you know how I feel about you then," he said without thinking. Maybe she didn't know. He looked out over the treetops down the street.

"I do Nicholas."

He heard his parents' car backing up the driveway, but he didn't look. He was too embarrassed. His parents probably thought he was silly.

"You know, we'll always be friends, Nicholas."

The tall moving guy walked across the grass toward Nicholas. He stopped at the door of the truck cab, opened it, got in, and slammed it shut. The immediate roar of the truck's engine starting made Nicholas take a step back. He stared at the tattered corner of his book as the truck drove off.

"So you got the stone and I got the book," he said, feeling stupid.

"Don't you want to be my friend?" Lucy asked. She moved closer to him. They both sat down cross-legged on the grass.

"Of course, silly he replied.

She smiled. They had reached a simple agreement. They both wanted the same thing. He already knew that, but saying it out loud would make it easier to part. He felt better suddenly. There was no real reason to feel bad, not really. He had the feeling he would see Lucy again before too long.

"Funny about the fish, huh?" he asked. He fingered the frayed corner of his book. Others must have touched the corner of the book many times before, maybe a long time ago and far far away.

Absentmindedly, he opened the book. In the center of the very first page was Lucy's symbol, three rings around a triangle. "Hey, look," he said. He showed her the picture.

"That's it, Nicholas!" Lucy squealed. "Oh my God. It's our symbol, the one that made you see the land with two suns." Nicholas took both her hands in his and closed his eyes.

"Kierdi gahsh mal," he said, the words popping out as if on their own.

"What did you say?" Lucy asked.

"It means when love takes flight," he said.

A gust of wind whipped around them like a dust devil without any dust. Lucy leaned into Nicholas. He could feel her close. His eyes were closed. Her long hair mixed with his in a tangle about his face and ears. He could feel her breathing close to him. The whirlwind had moved away, but he could still hear it whipping the elm tree outside his bedroom window. More of the strange but familiar words came suddenly to him.

"Chey enoi fala kem," he said.

Lucy squeezed his hands in response.

"Follow the spring of your heart," he interpreted. In his mind's eye, he saw the dark oval shaped silhouettes of two lovers standing on an open green plain, holding hands. Two suns, one orange and the other one red hung low in the greenish tinted sky. The stunning sunset lit up the most unusual lovers for a moment. They were not human at all. With their oblong shaped heads with their huge eyes, one on each side, they looked so much like the silken amber creature from the crystal clear pool. Nicholas knew somehow that the lovers were Lucy and he from another time and place. The image faded. He opened his eyes.

Lucy looked at him, but he could tell that she saw something far beyond him, something not of Emkhoura, not of Earth

"I saw it Nicholas, that place that you spoke of, the land with two suns. You and I were standing there in an open place together."

"I would love to go back there," he said, feeling a powerful longing that had always been buried deep inside him.

"We will," she said. "You just have to be patient."

Nicholas parent's drove up in their Pontiac and parked beside the curb, just behind Lucy. Nicholas couldn't see his parent's faces. He leaned toward Lucy as if it was the most natural thing in the world and kissed her on the lips. They hugged then, a tenderness and trust between them.

"I will miss you, Nicholas," Lucy said in his ear. When they came apart, both of them had tears in their eyes. Nicholas pulled Lucy up with him as he stood up from the cross-legged position.

"I'm going to write you, Lucy Lou," he said with a smile, one tear falling down to his cheek. "That'll be your nickname," he added.

Lucy smiled. Several tears streamed down her face. "Yeah and your nick name can be Nick, Nicknick."

"I like the sound of that," Nicholas said, dropping one of her hands, "Lucy Lou and Nicknick."

Nicholas rubbed her palm with his thumb a couple of times, and then dropped her hand as they both got up from the curb and walked toward the car.

He sat in the back seat and watched her out the side window of the car as they slowly drove away, then turned to look out the back window, as they got farther down the road. Lucy stood there on the grass, her long black hair blowing in the wind, her hand above her eyes to shade them from the sun.

Somewhere outside of town, Nicholas started to feel less sad. The car sped down the highway past the wheat fields of green, waving in the wind. He did so love the land. The hum of the car lulled him. All he could see of his parents in the front seat were the backs of their heads, necks, and shoulders. When would they ever come back to Flat Rock?

He'd learned so much from the land, the people, his dreams, and his new love. Life would never be the same. It would just keep changing and changing, a new chapter opening just when an old one closed. He saw a small blue spark of light near his hand, resting on his armrest.

The beautiful blue lights hardly lasted for more than a second before they disappeared. Each time he saw one of them, he felt another world opened, a kind of world so different that he wished he could see more of it.

"The Book of O" had mentioned the twelve dimensions of intergalactic learning. The blue lights must be a part of at least one of those dimensions. He'd always read about the three dimensions of length, width, and height. Maybe the blue lights were in the fourth dimension. Wouldn't it be something to see in all twelve dimensions? Boy, life was crazy, so much more so than most people imagined.

He had even learned some about the art of suffering. It seemed that he felt things more and suffered more, the longer he lived. The suffering made him appreciate the wonderful times that he could have. Even though he sometimes wanted life to stand still for the wrong reasons, it would go on. The Earth was such an amazing mystery.

He put his hand flat on "The Book of O" lying beside him on the seat. What would the book bring now? As he lifted it to his lap, it felt heavy, so much heavier. A peculiar feeling came over him as he opened the book to a middle page.

Curious symbols unlike any he'd ever seen filled the page (row after row of them, tiny picture writing of some sort that seemed to tell a story, describing something.) He turned the page and saw more of the writing. The hairs on the back of his neck stood up as he read the English interpretations beneath each line.

Tears fall into the ocean, one by one
Ten years, twenty, a thousand come and go.
Over the ages, we patiently wait
As each step taken brings us closer
To the timeless void of all that is.

The planets spin
Stars sparkle and dim
Yet we go onward
To the timeless void within.

Nicholas closed the book and laid it back down beside himself on the seat. Just as sure as he could see the green prairie pastures whizzing past beyond the barbed wire fence, he knew that when he looked back down the book would be gone. When he finally did look down, he smiled. "The Book of O" was gone, but it would never be forgotten.

If you'd like to leave me a message or comment:

https://www.facebook.com/martypriestart

opengate6@hotmail.com

ABOUT THE AUTHOR

https://www.facebook.com/martypriestart

Marty Priest lives in Kinsley, Kansas, a small town known as Midway USA, as it lies halfway between New York and San Francisco. Here in the heart of America on the Great Plains where the wind blows freely, he finds it is easy to think and create. Painting in oils and watercolor occupy much of his time, while his fondness for children and music inspire him to write stories and songs.

Made in the USA
Las Vegas, NV
22 April 2022